Monique and Dean
May 15, 2003
Verona, Italy

As You Like It

DOVER · THRIFT · EDITIONS

As You Like It

WILLIAM SHAKESPEARE

DOVER PUBLICATIONS, INC.
Mineola, New York

DOVER THRIFT EDITIONS

GENERAL EDITOR: PAUL NEGRI
EDITOR OF THIS VOLUME: SUSAN L. RATTINER

Bibliographical Note

This Dover edition, first published in 1998, contains the unabridged text of *As You Like It* as published in Volume V of *The Caxton Edition of the Complete Works of William Shakespeare*, Caxton Publishing Company, London, n.d. The Note was prepared specially for this edition, and explanatory footnotes from the Caxton edition have been revised.

Library of Congress Cataloging-in-Publication Data

Shakespeare, William, 1564–1616.
　　As you like it / William Shakespeare.
　　　　p.　cm. — (Dover thrift editions)
　　ISBN 0-486-40432-3 (pbk.)
　　I. Title.　II. Series.
PR2803.A1　1998
822.3'3—dc21
　　　　　　　　　　　　　　　　　　　　　　98-24631
　　　　　　　　　　　　　　　　　　　　　　CIP

Manufactured in the United States of America
Dover Publications, Inc., 31 East 2nd Street, Mineola, N.Y. 11501

Note

WILLIAM SHAKESPEARE (1564–1616) was born in Stratford-on-Avon, Warwickshire, England. He later moved to London to write for the theater. Shakespeare, joining an acting company known as the Lord Chamberlain's Men around 1594, received a share of the profits of his company's new playhouse. Averaging two plays per year, Shakespeare was also an actor, portraying such characters as the Ghost in *Hamlet* and Adam in *As You Like It*. Only eighteen of Shakespeare's plays were published during his lifetime. These plays, sold directly to theater companies, were often printed in quartos, or single-play editions without the author's approval.

As You Like It, one of Shakespeare's great comedies, was first published in 1623 in the collected edition of Shakespeare's plays known as the First Folio. Written sometime between 1599 and 1600, the play is based on *Rosalynde* (1590), a pastoral romance by Thomas Lodge. Shakespeare changed Lodge's euphuistic story into a satire involving disguises, mistaken identity, and love. With the addition of several new characters, such as Jaques, William, Touchstone, and Audrey, Shakespeare imbues the story with realism and humor. Similar in style to his earlier play, *Love's Labour's Lost* (1598), *As You Like It* focuses on the dramatic elements of characterization and dialogue. The play's woodland setting is established almost at once, allowing the audience to appreciate the charms of nature and the outdoors.

Written specifically for performance, the plays of William Shakespeare drew popular audiences both in his own day and to the present day. As a playwright, Shakespeare was able to accurately gauge the dramatic import of a scene and fill it with memorable prose and verse. His literary mastery remains unequaled; his plays are performed continually around the world.

Contents

Dramatis Personæ[1]

DUKE, living in banishment.
FREDERICK, his brother, and usurper of his dominions.
AMIENS, ⎫
JAQUES, ⎭ lords attending on the banished Duke.
LE BEAU, a courtier attending upon Frederick.
CHARLES, wrestler to Frederick.
OLIVER, ⎫
JAQUES, ⎬ sons of Sir Rowland de Boys.
ORLANDO, ⎭
ADAM, ⎫
DENNIS, ⎭ servants to Oliver.
TOUCHSTONE, a clown.
SIR OLIVER MARTEXT, a vicar.
CORIN, ⎫
SYLVIUS, ⎭ shepherds.
WILLIAM, a country fellow, in love with Audrey.
A person representing Hymen.

ROSALIND, daughter to the banished Duke.
CELIA, daughter to Frederick.
PHEBE, a shepherdess.
AUDREY, a country wench.

Lords, pages, and attendants, &c.

SCENE—*Oliver's house; Duke Frederick's court; and the Forest of Arden*

[1]This play, which was first printed in the First Folio in 1623, is there divided into acts and scenes. There is no list of *Dramatis Personæ*. This was supplied for the first time in Rowe's edition of 1709.

ACT I.

SCENE I. *Orchard of Oliver's House.*

Enter ORLANDO *and* ADAM

ORLANDO.   As I remember, Adam, it was upon this fashion: bequeathed me[1] by will but poor a thousand crowns, and, as thou
sayest, charged my brother, on his blessing, to breed me well: and
there begins my sadness. My brother Jaques[2] he keeps at school,
and report speaks goldenly of his profit: for my part, he keeps me
rustically at home, or, to speak more properly, stays me here at
home unkept; for call you that keeping for a gentleman of my
birth, that differs not from the stalling of an ox? His horses are bred
better; for, besides that they are fair with their feeding, they are
taught their manage, and to that end riders dearly hired: but I, his
brother, gain nothing under him but growth; for the which his animals on his dunghills are as much bound to him as I. Besides this
nothing that he so plentifully gives me, the something that nature
gave me his countenance[3] seems to take from me: he lets me feed
with his hinds, bars me the place of a brother, and, as much as in

---

[1] *bequeathed me, etc.*] This sentence lacks a subject. It is possible that "he" was omitted
before "bequeathed" by a typographical error. It is so obvious that Orlando is talking
of his father's bequest that a corrector of the press could not be severely blamed for the
accidental elision.

[2] *My brother Jaques*] This character, Sir Rowland de Boys' second son, only plays a small
part at the end of the last act, where the folio editions call him "second brother" and
Rowe and later editors "Jaques de Boys." In Lodge's story of *Rosalynd*, on which
Shakespeare based his play, the character is called Ferdinand. That Shakespeare
should have bestowed the same name on a far more important personage of his own
creation, the banished Duke's cynical companion, is proof of hasty composition and of
defective revision. Cf. note on I, ii, 74, *infra.*

[3] *countenance*] Cf. Selden's *Table Talk* (Art. "Fines"): "If you will come unto my house,
I will show you the best *countenance* I can," *i.e.* not the best face, but the best
entertainment.

1

him lies, mines my gentility with my education.[4] This is it, Adam, that grieves me; and the spirit of my father, which I think is within me, begins to mutiny against this servitude: I will no longer endure it, though yet I know no wise remedy how to avoid it.

ADAM.   Yonder comes my master, your brother.

ORL.   Go apart, Adam, and thou shalt hear how he will shake me up.

Enter OLIVER

OLI.   Now, sir! what make you here?

ORL.   Nothing: I am not taught to make any thing.

OLI.   What mar you then, sir?

ORL.   Marry, sir, I am helping you to mar that which God made, a poor unworthy brother of yours, with idleness.

OLI.   Marry, sir, be better employed, and be naught awhile.[5]

ORL.   Shall I keep your hogs and eat husks with them? What prodigal portion have I spent, that I should come to such penury?

OLI.   Know you where you are, sir?

ORL.   O, sir, very well; here in your orchard.

OLI.   Know you before whom, sir?

ORL.   Ay, better than him I am before knows me. I know you are my eldest brother; and, in the gentle condition of blood, you should so know me. The courtesy of nations allows you my better, in that you are the firstborn; but the same tradition takes not away my blood, were there twenty brothers betwixt us: I have as much of my father in me as you; albeit, I confess, your coming before me is nearer to his reverence.[6]

OLI.   What, boy!

ORL.   Come, come, elder brother, you are too young in this.[7]

OLI.   Wilt thou lay hands on me, villain?

ORL.   I am no villain; I am the youngest son of Sir Rowland de Boys; he was my father, and he is thrice a villain that says such a father begot villains. Wert thou not my brother, I would not take this hand from thy throat till this other had pulled out thy tongue for saying so: thou hast railed on thyself.

---

[4]*mines . . . education*] undermines or destroys the gentleness of my birth and nature, by means of my bringing up.

[5]*be naught awhile*] a colloquial form of imprecation, "be hanged to you."

[6]*your coming . . . reverence*] your priority of birth more closely associates you with the respect which was his due. The chief share of the father's reputation descends to his eldest born.

[7]*Come, come . . . young in this*] Cf. the elder brother's remark in Lodge's story of *Rosalynd*, "Though I am *eldest* by birth, yet never having attempted any deeds of arms, I am *youngest* to perform any martial exploits."

ADAM.   Sweet masters, be patient: for your father's remembrance, be at accord.

OLI.   Let me go, I say.

ORL.   I will not, till I please: you shall hear me. My father charged you in his will to give me good education: you have trained me like a peasant, obscuring and hiding from me all gentleman-like qualities. The spirit of my father grows strong in me, and I will no longer endure it: therefore allow me such exercises as may become a gentleman, or give me the poor allottery my father left me by testament; with that I will go buy my fortunes.

OLI.   And what wilt thou do? beg, when that is spent? Well, sir, get you in: I will not long be troubled with you; you shall have some part of your will: I pray you, leave me.

ORL.   I will no further offend you than becomes me for my good.

OLI.   Get you with him, you old dog.

ADAM.   Is "old dog" my reward?? Most true, I have lost my teeth in your service. God be with my old master! he would not have spoke such a word.

[*Exeunt* ORLANDO *and* ADAM.

OLI.   Is it even so? begin you to grow upon me? I will physic your rankness, and yet give no thousand crowns neither. Holla, Dennis!

Enter DENNIS

DEN.   Calls your worship?

OLI.   Was not Charles, the Duke's wrestler, here to speak with me?

DEN.   So please you, he is here at the door and importunes access to you.

OLI.   Call him in. [*Exit* DENNIS.] 'T will be a good way; and to-morrow the wrestling is.

Enter CHARLES

CHA.   Good morrow to your worship.

OLI.   Good Monsieur Charles, what's the new news at the new court?

CHA.   There's no news at the court, sir, but the old news: that is, the old Duke is banished by his younger brother the new Duke; and three or four loving lords have put themselves into voluntary exile with him, whose lands and revenues enrich the new Duke; therefore he gives them good leave to wander.

OLI.   Can you tell if Rosalind, the Duke's daughter, be banished with her father?

CHA.   O, no; for the Duke's daughter, her cousin, so loves her, being ever from their cradles bred together, that she would have followed her exile, or have died to stay behind her. She is at the court, and no less beloved of her uncle than his own daughter; and never two ladies loved as they do.

OLI. Where will the old Duke live?

CHA. They say he is already in the forest of Arden,[8] and a many merry men with him; and there they live like the old Robin Hood of England: they say many young gentlemen flock to him every day, and fleet the time carelessly, as they did in the golden world.

OLI. What, you wrestle to-morrow before the new Duke?

CHA. Marry, do I, sir; and I came to acquaint you with a matter. I am given, sir, secretly to understand that your younger brother, Orlando, hath a disposition to come in disguised against me to try a fall. To-morrow, sir, I wrestle for my credit; and he that escapes me without some broken limb shall acquit him well. Your brother is but young and tender; and, for your love, I would be loath to foil him, as I must, for my own honour, if he come in: therefore, out of my love to you, I came hither to acquaint you withal; that either you might stay him from his intendment, or brook such disgrace well as he shall run into; in that it is a thing of his own search, and altogether against my will.

OLI. Charles, I thank thee for thy love to me, which thou shalt find I will most kindly requite. I had myself notice of my brother's purpose herein, and have by underhand means laboured to dissuade him from it, but he is resolute. I'll tell thee, Charles:—it is the stubbornest young fellow of France; full of ambition, an envious emulator of every man's good parts, a secret and villanous contriver against me his natural brother: therefore use thy discretion; I had as lief thou didst break his neck as his finger. And thou wert best look to 't; for if thou dost him any slight disgrace, or if he do not mightily grace himself on thee,[9] he will practise against thee by poison, entrap thee by some treacherous device, and never leave thee till he hath ta'en thy life by some indirect means or other; for, I assure thee, and almost with tears I speak it, there is not one so young and so villanous this day living. I speak but brotherly of him; but should I anatomize him to thee as he is, I must blush and weep, and thou must look pale and wonder.

CHA. I am heartily glad I came hither to you. If he come to-morrow, I'll give him his payment: if ever he go alone again, I'll never wrestle for prize more: and so, God keep your worship!

---

[8]*forest of Arden*] Lodge, like Shakespeare, makes the scene of his story "the forest of Ardennes," in Flanders (now Belgium). But the dramatist's familiarity with the English forest of Arden in Warwickshire, near his native town of Stratford-on-Avon, probably coloured his allusions to woodland scenery in the play.

[9]*grace himself on thee*] get grace or honour at your expense.

OLI. Farewell, good Charles. [*Exit* CHARLES.] Now will I stir this gamester: I hope I shall see an end of him; for my soul, yet I know not why, hates nothing more than he. Yet he's gentle; never schooled, and yet learned; full of noble device;[10] of all sorts enchantingly beloved; and indeed so much in the heart of the world, and especially of my own people, who best know him, that I am altogether misprised: but it shall not be so long; this wrestler shall clear all: nothing remains but that I kindle the boy thither; which now I'll go about.   [*Exit.*

SCENE II. *Lawn Before the Duke's Palace.*

Enter ROSALIND *and* CELIA

CEL. I pray thee, Rosalind, sweet my coz, be merry.

ROS. Dear Celia, I show more mirth than I am mistress of; and would you yet I were merrier? Unless you could teach me to forget a banished father, you must not learn me how to remember any extraordinary pleasure.

CEL. Herein I see thou lovest me not with the full weight that I love thee. If my uncle, thy banished father, had banished thy uncle, the Duke my father, so thou hadst been still with me, I could have taught my love to take thy father for mine: so wouldst thou, if the truth of thy love to me were so righteously tempered as mine is to thee.

ROS. Well, I will forget the condition of my estate, to rejoice in yours.

CEL. You know my father hath no child but I, nor none is like to have: and, truly, when he dies, thou shalt be his heir; for what he hath taken away from thy father perforce, I will render thee again in affection; by mine honour, I will; and when I break that oath, let me turn monster: therefore, my sweet Rose, my dear Rose, be merry.

ROS. From henceforth I will, coz, and devise sports. Let me see; what think you of falling in love?

CEL. Marry, I prithee, do, to make sport withal: but love no man in good earnest; nor no further in sport neither, than with safety of a pure blush thou mayst in honour come off again.

ROS. What shall be our sport, then?

---

[10]*noble device*] noble conceptions and aims.

CEL.   Let us sit and mock the good housewife Fortune from her wheel,[1] that her gifts may henceforth be bestowed equally.

ROS.   I would we could do so; for her benefits are mightily misplaced; and the bountiful blind woman doth most mistake in her gifts to women.

CEL.   'T is true; for those that she makes fair she scarce makes honest; and those that she makes honest she makes very ill-favouredly.

ROS.   Nay, now thou goest from Fortune's office to Nature's: Fortune reigns in gifts of the world, not in the lineaments of Nature.

Enter TOUCHSTONE

CEL.   No? when Nature hath made a fair creature, may she not by Fortune fall into the fire? Though Nature hath given us wit to flout at Fortune, hath not Fortune sent in this fool to cut off the argument?

ROS.   Indeed, there is Fortune too hard for Nature, when Fortune makes Nature's natural the cutter-off of Nature's wit.

CEL.   Peradventure this is not Fortune's work neither, but Nature's; who perceiveth our natural wits too dull to reason of[2] such goddesses, and hath sent this natural for our whetstone; for always the dulness of the fool is the whetstone of the wits. How now, wit! whither wander you?[3]

TOUCH.   Mistress, you must come away to your father.

CEL.   Were you made the messenger?

TOUCH.   No, by mine honour, but I was bid to come for you.

ROS.   Where learned you that oath, fool?

TOUCH.   Of a certain knight that swore by his honour they were good pancakes, and swore by his honour the mustard was naught; now I'll stand to it, the pancakes were naught and the mustard was good, and yet was not the knight forsworn.

CEL.   How prove you that, in the great heap of your knowledge?

ROS.   Ay, marry, now unmuzzle your wisdom.

TOUCH.   Stand you both forth now: stroke your chins, and swear by your beards that I am a knave.

CEL.   By our beards, if we had them, thou art.

TOUCH.   By my knavery, if I had it, then I were; but if you swear by that that is not, you are not forsworn: no more was this knight, swearing by his honour, for he never had any; or if he had, he had sworn it away before ever he saw those pancakes or that mustard.

---

[1]*Fortune . . . wheel*] Cf. *Hen. V*, III, vi, 32–34: "*Fortune* is painted . . . with a *wheel*, to signify to you, which is the moral of it, that she is turning, and inconstant, and mutability, and variation."

[2]*reason of*] discuss about. Cf. *Merch. of Ven.*, I, iii, 54, "I am debating *of* my present store," and *ibid.* II, viii, 27, "I *reasoned with* a Frenchman yesterday."

[3]*wit! whither wander you?*] a proverbial phrase serving as a check on too abundant a flow of conversation. The cognate form IV, i, 149, *infra*, "Wit! whither wilt?" is more frequently met with. Malone conjectured that the words formed part of some lost madrigal.

CEL.　Prithee, who is 't that thou meanest?

TOUCH.　One that old Frederick, your father,[4] loves.

CEL.　My father's love is enough to honour him: enough! speak no more of him; you'll be whipped for taxation one of these days.

TOUCH.　The more pity, that fools may not speak wisely what wise men do foolishly.

CEL.　By my troth, thou sayest true; for since the little wit that fools have was silenced, the little foolery that wise men have makes a great show.[5] Here comes Monsieur Le Beau.

ROS.　With his mouth full of news.

CEL.　Which he will put on us, as pigeons feed their young.

ROS.　Then shall we be news-crammed.

CEL.　All the better; we shall be the more marketable.

Enter LE BEAU

Bon jour, Monsieur Le Beau: what's the news?

LE BEAU.　Fair princess, you have lost much good sport.

CEL.　Sport! of what colour?[6]

LE BEAU.　What colour, madam! how shall I answer you?

ROS.　As wit and fortune will.

TOUCH.　Or as the Destinies decrees.

CEL.　Well said: that was laid on with a trowel.

TOUCH.　Nay, if I keep not my rank, —

ROS.　Thou losest thy old smell.[7]

LE BEAU.　You amaze me, ladies: I would have told you of good wrestling, which you have lost the sight of.

ROS.　Yet tell us the manner of the wrestling.

LE BEAU.　I will tell you the beginning; and, if it please your ladyships,

---

[4]*old Frederick, your father*] The reference here must be to Celia's father, the usurping Duke, who at line 213 of the present scene and at V, iv, 148, *infra*, is also called Frederick. Yet the Folios give the succeeding speech to *Rosalind*, and thereby imply that Touchstone refers here to Rosalind's father, the banished Duke, who is designated throughout the play as "Duke, senior," without any Christian name; it is clear that his name could not have been Frederick, like that of his brother. Capell, who accepted the Folios' assignment of the next speech to Rosalind, substituted Ferdinand for Frederick. But it is best to adopt Theobald's emendation, which is followed above, and assign the next speech to Celia.

[5]*since . . . great show*] There may be a reference here to some topical event, either to an unidentified inhibition of players, or to the notorious suppression of satirical and licentious books, which took place in 1599.

[6]*colour*] kind or nature. Cf. *Lear*, II, ii, 133, where the Quartos read "a fellow of the self-same *nature*," and the Folio, "a fellow of the self-same *colour*."

[7]*rank . . . smell*] This punning comment on the word "rank," which Touchstone uses in its sense of "quality" or "place," and Rosalind in that of "rancidity," is precisely paralleled in *Cymb.*, II, i, 15–16: "CLO. Would he had been one of my *rank*! SEC. LORD [*Aside*]. To have *smelt* like a fool."

you may see the end; for the best is yet to do; and here, where you are, they are coming to perform it.

CEL. Well, the beginning, that is dead and buried.

LE BEAU. There comes an old man and his three sons,—

CEL. I could match this beginning with an old tale.

LE BEAU. Three proper young men, of excellent growth and presence.

ROS. With bills on their necks,[8] "Be it known unto all men by these presents."

LE BEAU. The eldest of the three wrestled with Charles, the Duke's wrestler; which Charles in a moment threw him, and broke three of his ribs, that there is little hope of life in him: so he served the second, and so the third. Yonder they lie; the poor old man, their father, making such pitiful dole over them that all the beholders take his part with weeping.

ROS. Alas!

TOUCH. But what is the sport, monsieur, that the ladies have lost?

LE BEAU. Why, this that I speak of.

TOUCH. Thus men may grow wiser every day: it is the first time that ever I heard breaking of ribs was sport for ladies.

CEL. Or I, I promise thee.

ROS. But is there any else longs to see this broken music[9] in his sides? is there yet another dotes upon rib-breaking? Shall we see this wrestling, cousin?

LE BEAU. You must, if you stay here; for here is the place appointed for the wrestling, and they are ready to perform it.

CEL. Yonder, sure, they are coming: let us now stay and see it.

Flourish. Enter DUKE FREDERICK, LORDS, ORLANDO, CHARLES, *and* Attendants

DUKE F. Come on: since the youth will not be entreated, his own peril on his forwardness.

ROS. Is yonder the man?

LE BEAU. Even he, madam.

CEL. Alas, he is too young! yet he looks successfully.

DUKE F. How now, daughter and cousin! are you crept hither to see the wrestling?

---

[8]*Ros. With bills on their necks*] Thus the Folios. Farmer transferred these words to Le Beau's preceding speech, and interpreted them as meaning "with halberds, or weapons of war, on their shoulders." Lodge in the novel writes of his hero "with his forest *bill on his neck.*" In any case Rosalind puns on the word "bills" [*i.e.* halberds] in the sense of placards or proclamations.

[9]*broken music*] A quibbling use of a technical musical term for a musical performance, in which the instruments employed did not keep tune, according to strict rules of harmony. There is no connection between broken music and broken ribs, save the verbal identity of the epithet.

Ros.   Ay, my liege, so please you give us leave.

Duke F.   You will take little delight in it, I can tell you, there is such odds in the man.[10] In pity of the challenger's youth I would fain dissuade him, but he will not be entreated. Speak to him, ladies; see if you can move him.

Cel.   Call him hither, good Monsieur Le Beau.

Duke F.   Do so: I'll not be by.

Le Beau.   Monsieur the challenger, the princess calls[11] for you.

Orl.   I attend them with all respect and duty.

Ros.   Young man, have you challenged Charles the wrestler?

Orl.   No, fair princess; he is the general challenger: I come but in, as others do, to try with him the strength of my youth.

Cel.   Young gentleman, your spirits are too bold for your years. You have seen cruel proof of this man's strength: if you saw yourself with your eyes, or knew yourself with your judgement,[12] the fear of your adventure would counsel you to a more equal enterprise. We pray you, for your own sake, to embrace your own safety, and give over this attempt.

Ros.   Do, young sir; your reputation shall not therefore be misprised: we will make it our suit to the Duke that the wrestling might not go forward.

Orl.   I beseech you, punish me not with your hard thoughts; wherein I confess me much guilty, to deny so fair and excellent ladies any thing. But let your fair eyes and gentle wishes go with me to my trial: wherein if I be foiled, there is but one shamed that was never gracious; if killed, but one dead that is willing to be so: I shall do my friends no wrong, for I have none to lament me; the world no injury, for in it I have nothing: only in the world I fill up a place, which may be better supplied when I have made it empty.

Ros.   The little strength that I have, I would it were with you.

Cel.   And mine, to eke out hers.

Ros.   Fare you well: pray heaven I be deceived in you!

Cel.   Your heart's desires be with you!

Cha.   Come, where is this young gallant that is so desirous to lie with his mother earth?

Orl.   Ready, sir; but his will hath in it a more modest working.

Duke F.   You shall try but one fall.

Cha.   No, I warrant your Grace, you shall not entreat him to a second, that have so mightily persuaded him from a first.

---

[10]*odds in the man*] advantage on the side of the wrestler Charles.

[11]*princess calls*] Theobald reads *princesses call*, which Orlando's reference to *them* seems to justify.

[12]*saw . . . judgement*] exerted all your powers of vision and judgment.

ORL.   You mean to mock me after; you should not have mocked me
    before: but come your ways.
ROS.   Now Hercules be thy speed, young man!
CEL.   I would I were invisible, to catch the strong fellow by the leg.
                                [They wrestle.

ROS.   O excellent young man!
CEL.   If I had a thunderbolt in mine eye, I can tell who should down.
                        [Shout. Charles is thrown.
DUKE F.   No more, no more.
ORL.   Yes, I beseech your Grace: I am not yet well breathed.[13]
DUKE F.   How dost thou, Charles?
LE BEAU.   He cannot speak, my lord.
DUKE F.   Bear him away. What is thy name, young man?
ORL.   Orlando, my liege; the youngest son of Sir Rowland de Boys.
DUKE F.   I would thou hadst been son to some man else:
    The world esteem'd thy father honourable,
    But I did find him still mine enemy:
    Thou shouldst have better pleased me with this deed,
    Hadst thou descended from another house.
    But fare thee well; thou art a gallant youth:
    I would thou hadst told me of another father.
               [Exeunt DUKE FRED., *train, and* LE BEAU.
CEL.   Were I my father, coz, would I do this?
ORL.   I am more proud to be Sir Rowland's son,
    His youngest son; and would not change that calling,[14]
    To be adopted heir to Frederick.
ROS.   My father loved Sir Rowland as his soul,
    And all the world was of my father's mind:
    Had I before known this young man his son,
    I should have given him tears unto entreaties,[15]
    Ere he should thus have ventured.
CEL.   Gentle cousin,
    Let us go thank him and encourage him:
    My father's rough and envious disposition
    Sticks me at heart. Sir, you have well deserved:
    If you do keep your promises in love
    But justly, as you have exceeded all promise,
    Your mistress shall be happy.

---

[13]*not yet well breathed*] not yet in thorough practice, in full career. Cf. *Ant. and Cleop.,*
    III, xiii, 178: "I will be treble-sinewed, hearted, *breathed.*"
[14]*calling*] name, or appellation. This usage is rare. The word is more common in
    Shakespeare in the modern sense of "vocation" or "profession," especially of an ec-
    clesiastical kind.
[15]*tears unto entreaties*] tears in addition to entreaties.

ROS.   Gentleman,
                       [*Giving him a chain from her neck.*
    Wear this for me, one out of suits with fortune,[16]
    That could give more, but that her hand lacks means.
    Shall we go, coz?
CEL.   Ay. Fare you well, fair gentleman.
ORL.   Can I not say, I thank you? My better parts
    Are all thrown down, and that which here stands up
    Is but a quintain, a mere lifeless block.
ROS.   He calls us back: my pride fell with my fortunes;
    I'll ask him what he would. Did you call, sir?
    Sir, you have wrestled well and overthrown
    More than your enemies.
CEL.   Will you go, coz?
ROS.   Have with you. Fare you well.   [*Exeunt* ROSALIND *and* CELIA.
ORL.   What passion hangs these weights upon my tongue?
    I cannot speak to her, yet she urged conference.
    O poor Orlando, thou art overthrown!
    Or Charles or something weaker masters thee.

Re-enter LE BEAU

LE BEAU.   Good sir, I do in friendship counsel you
    To leave this place. Albeit you have deserved
    High commendation, true applause, and love,
    Yet such is now the Duke's condition,[17]
    That he misconstrues all that you have done.
    The Duke is humorous: what he is, indeed,
    More suits you to conceive than I to speak of.
ORL.   I thank you, sir: and, pray you, tell me this,
    Which of the two was daughter of the Duke,
    That here was at the wrestling?
LE BEAU.   Neither his daughter, if we judge by manners;
    But yet, indeed, the taller[18] is his daughter:
    The other is daughter to the banish'd Duke,
    And here detain'd by her usurping uncle,

---

[16]*out of suits with fortune*] out of fortune's service, deprived of her livery. Cf. I, iii, 24, *infra*: "turning these jests *out of service.*"

[17]*condition*] temperament. Cf. *Merch. of Ven.*, I, ii, 143: "*the condition* [*i.e.* temperament or disposition] of a saint."

[18]*taller*] This is the reading of the Folios. Rowe and almost all subsequent editors read here *shorter* (or *smaller*). A change of the kind seems necessary. Rosalind, in the next scene, line 110, gives as a reason for her assuming a man's disguise when fleeing with Celia that she is "more than common tall," and at IV, iii, 86–87, Celia is described as "low and browner" than Rosalind.

    To keep his daughter company; whose loves
    Are dearer than the natural bond of sisters.
    But I can tell you that of late this Duke
    Hath ta'en displeasure 'gainst his gentle niece,
    Grounded upon no other argument
    But that the people praise her for her virtues,
    And pity her for her good father's sake;
    And, on my life, his malice 'gainst the lady
    Will suddenly break forth. Sir, fare you well.
    Hereafter, in a better world than this,
    I shall desire more love and knowledge of you.
ORL.   I rest much bounden to you: fare you well.   [*Exit* LE BEAU.
    Thus must I from the smoke into the smother;[19]
    From tyrant Duke unto a tyrant brother:
    But heavenly Rosalind!   [*Exit.*

SCENE III. *A Room in the Palace.*

Enter CELIA *and* ROSALIND

CEL.   Why, cousin! why, Rosalind! Cupid have mercy! not a word?
ROS.   Not one to throw at a dog.
CEL.   No, thy words are too precious to be cast away upon curs; throw
    some of them at me; come, lame me with reasons.
ROS.   Then there were two cousins laid up; when the one should be
    lamed with reasons and the other mad without any.
CEL.   But is all this for your father?
ROS.   No, some of it is for my child's father.[1] O, how full of briers is
    this working-day world!
CEL.   They are but burs, cousin, thrown upon thee in holiday foolery: if
    we walk not in the trodden paths, our very petticoats will catch them.
ROS.   I could shake them off my coat: these burs are in my heart.
CEL.   Hem[2] them away.

---

[19]*from the smoke . . . smother*] from bad to worse. "Smother" is the thick stifling smoke
  of a smouldering fire.

[1]*my child's father*] this would mean "my husband." Thus the Folios. Numerous modern
  editors substitute *my father's child, i.e.* myself.
[2]*Hem*] an onomatopœic word implying the act of coughing slightly. "Hem them away"
  is remove them by a small effort of the throat.

Ros.   I would try, if I could cry hem and have him.[3]

Cel.   Come, come, wrestle with thy affections.

Ros.   O, they take the part of a better wrestler than myself!

Cel.   O, a good wish upon you! you will try in time, in despite of a fall. But, turning these jests out of service, let us talk in good earnest: is it possible, on such a sudden, you should fall into so strong a liking with old Sir Rowland's youngest son?

Ros.   The Duke my father loved his father dearly.

Cel.   Doth it therefore ensue that you should love his son dearly? By this kind of chase, I should hate him, for my father hated his father dearly;[4] yet I hate not Orlando.

Ros.   No, faith, hate him not, for my sake.

Cel.   Why should I not? doth he not deserve well?

Ros.   Let me love him for that, and do you love him because I do. Look, here comes the Duke.

Cel.   With his eyes full of anger.

Enter Duke Frederick, *with* Lords

Duke F.   Mistress, dispatch you with your safest[5] haste
And get you from our court.

Ros.   Me, uncle?

Duke F.   You, cousin:
Within these ten days if that thou be'st found
So near our public court as twenty miles,
Thou diest for it.

Ros.   I do beseech your Grace,
Let me the knowledge of my fault bear with me:
If with myself I hold intelligence,
Or have acquaintance with mine own desires;
If that I do not dream, or be not frantic,—
As I do trust I am not,—then, dear uncle,
Never so much as in a thought unborn
Did I offend your Highness.

Duke F.   Thus do all traitors:
If their purgation did consist in words,
They are as innocent as grace itself:
Let it suffice thee that I trust thee not.

Ros.   Yet your mistrust cannot make me a traitor:
Tell me whereon the likelihood depends.

Duke F.   Thou art thy father's daughter; there's enough.

---

[3]*cry hem and have him*] have for the asking; a proverbial expression.
[4]*dearly*] greatly, extremely. Cf. *Hamlet*, I, ii, 182: "my *dearest* foe."
[5]*safest*] surest, least exposed to doubt or delay.

ROS.　So was I when your Highness took his dukedom;
　　　So was I when your Highness banish'd him:
　　　Treason is not inherited, my lord;
　　　Or, if we did derive it from our friends,
　　　What's that to me? my father was no traitor:
　　　Then, good my liege, mistake me not so much
　　　To think my poverty is treacherous.
CEL.　Dear sovereign, hear me speak.
DUKE F.　Ay, Celia; we stay'd her for your sake,
　　　Else had she with her father ranged along.
CEL.　I did not then entreat to have her stay;
　　　It was your pleasure and your own remorse:
　　　I was too young that time to value her;
　　　But now I know her: if she be a traitor,
　　　Why so am I; we still have slept together,
　　　Rose at an instant, learn'd, play'd, eat together,
　　　And wheresoe'er we went, like Juno's swans,[6]
　　　Still we went coupled and inseparable.
DUKE F.　She is too subtle for thee; and her smoothness,
　　　Her very silence and her patience
　　　Speak to the people, and they pity her.
　　　Thou art a fool: she robs thee of thy name;
　　　And thou wilt show more bright and seem more virtuous
　　　When she is gone. Then open not thy lips:
　　　Firm and irrevocable is my doom
　　　Which I have pass'd upon her; she is banish'd.
CEL.　Pronounce that sentence then on me, my liege:
　　　I cannot live out of her company.
DUKE F.　You are a fool. You, niece, provide yourself:
　　　If you outstay the time, upon mine honour,
　　　And in the greatness of my word, you die.
　　　　　　　　　　　[*Exeunt* DUKE FREDERICK *and* Lords.
CEL.　O my poor Rosalind, whither wilt thou go?
　　　Wilt thou change fathers? I will give thee mine.
　　　I charge thee, be not thou more grieved than I am.
ROS.　I have more cause.
CEL.　　　　　　　　Thou hast not, cousin;
　　　Prithee, be cheerful: know'st thou not, the Duke
　　　Hath banish'd me, his daughter?

---

[6]*like Juno's swans*] There is nothing in classical mythology to justify this simile, which seems due to an error of memory. Ovid associates *Venus* and *not Juno* with swans. Cf. *Met.*, X, 708 *seq.* Shakespeare mentions "Venus' doves" seven times in the course of his works, but he ignores her swans.

Ros.   That he hath not.
Cel.   No, hath not? Rosalind lacks then the love
        Which teacheth thee that thou and I am one:
        Shall we be sunder'd? shall we part, sweet girl?
        No: let my father seek another heir.
        Therefore devise with me how we may fly,
        Whither to go and what to bear with us;
        And do not seek to take your change[7] upon you,
        To bear your griefs yourself and leave me out;
        For, by this heaven, now at our sorrows pale,
        Say what thou canst, I'll go along with thee.
Ros.   Why, whither shall we go?
Cel.   To seek my uncle in the forest of Arden.
Ros.   Alas, what danger will it be to us,
        Maids as we are, to travel forth so far!
        Beauty provoketh thieves sooner than gold.
Cel.   I'll put myself in poor and mean attire
        And with a kind of umber smirch my face;
        The like do you: so shall we pass along
        And never stir assailants.
Ros.   Were it not better,
        Because that I am more than common tall,
        That I did suit me all points like a man?
        A gallant curtle-axe upon my thigh,
        A boar-spear in my hand; and—in my heart
        Lie there what hidden woman's fear there will—
        We'll have a swashing and a martial outside,
        As many other mannish cowards have
        That do outface it with their semblances.
Cel.   What shall I call thee when thou art a man?
Ros.   I'll have no worse a name than Jove's own page;
        And therefore look you call me Ganymede.
        But what will you be call'd?
Cel.   Something that hath a reference to my state;
        No longer Celia, but Aliena.
Ros.   But, cousin, what if we assay'd to steal
        The clownish fool out of your father's court?
        Would he not be a comfort to our travel?
Cel.   He'll go along o'er the wide world with me;
        Leave me alone to woo him. Let's away,

---

[7]*your change*] For this reading of the First Folio the Second and later Folios substituted
your charge, which seems to improve the sense. But the original reading *change, i.e.*
"reverse of fortune," may be right.

And get our jewels and our wealth together;
Devise the fittest time and safest way
To hide us from pursuit that will be made
After my flight. Now go we in content
To liberty and not to banishment.   [*Exeunt.*

ACT II.

Scene I. *The Forest of Arden.*

Enter Duke Senior, Amiens, *and two or three* Lords, *like foresters*

Duke S.   Now, my co-mates and brothers in exile,
          Hath not old custom made this life more sweet
          Than that of painted pomp?
          Are not these woods
          More free from peril than the envious court?
          Here feel we but the penalty of Adam,
          The seasons' difference; as the icy fang
          And churlish chiding of the winter's wind,
          Which, when it bites and blows upon my body,
          Even till I shrink with cold, I smile and say
          "This is no flattery: these are counsellors
          That feelingly persuade me what I am."
          Sweet are the uses of adversity;
          Which, like the toad, ugly and venomous,
          Wears yet a precious jewel in his head:[1]
          And this our life exempt from public haunt
          Finds tongues in trees, books in the running brooks,
          Sermons in stones and good in every thing.
          I would not change it.
Ami.   Happy is your Grace,

[1] *precious jewel in his head*] Cf. Lyly's *Euphues:* "The foule Toade hath a faire stone in his head" (ed. Arber, p. 53). The ignorant popular belief, that a toad carried a precious stone in its head, which was universal in Shakespeare's day, is apparently derived from the fact that a stone or gem, chiefly found in Egypt, is of the brownish gray colour of toads, and is therefore called a batrachite or toadstone. Pliny in his *Natural History* (Book 32) ascribes to a bone in the toad's head curative and other properties, but does not suggest that a gem is ever found there. In his description elsewhere of the toad-stones of Egypt he only notes their association with toads in the way of colour.

That can translate the stubbornness of fortune
Into so quiet and so sweet a style.
DUKE S.   Come, shall we go and kill us venison?
And yet it irks me the poor dappled fools,
Being native burghers of this desert city,
Should in their own confines with forked heads[2]
Have their round haunches gored.
FIRST LORD.   Indeed, my lord,
The melancholy Jaques grieves at that,
And, in that kind, swears you do more usurp
Than doth your brother that hath banish'd you.
To-day my Lord of Amiens and myself
Did steal behind him as he lay along
Under an oak whose antique root peeps out
Upon the brook that brawls along this wood:
To the which place a poor sequester'd stag,
That from the hunter's aim had ta'en a hurt,
Did come to languish, and indeed, my lord,
The wretched animal heaved forth such groans,
That their discharge did stretch his leathern coat
Almost to bursting, and the big round tears
Coursed one another down his innocent nose
In piteous chase; and thus the hairy fool,
Much marked of the melancholy Jaques,
Stood on the extremest verge of the swift brook,
Augmenting it with tears.
DUKE S.   But what said Jaques?
Did he not moralize[3] this spectacle?
FIRST LORD.   O, yes, into a thousand similes.
First, for his weeping into the needless stream;
"Poor deer," quoth he, "thou makest a testament
As worldlings do, giving thy sum of more
To that which had too much": then, being there alone,
Left and abandon'd of his velvet friends;
"'T is right," quoth he; "thus misery doth part
The flux of company": anon a careless herd,
Full of the pasture, jumps along by him
And never stays to greet him; "Ay," quoth Jaques,

---

[2]*forked heads*] arrow heads. Roger Ascham, in *Toxophilus* (ed. Arber, p. 135), mentions that arrow heads, "having two points stretching forwards," are commonly called "fork heads." Cf. *Lear*, I, i, 143, where the arrow-head is called "the fork."
[3]*moralize*] Cf. Cotgrave, *Fr.-Eng. Dict.*: "Moraliser: To *morralize*, to expound morrally, to give a morall sence vnto." See also *infra*, II, vii, 29: "*moral* on the time."

"Sweep on, you fat and greasy citizens;
'T is just the fashion: wherefore do you look
Upon that poor and broken bankrupt there?"
Thus most invectively he pierceth through
The body of the country, city, court,
Yea, and of this our life; swearing that we
Are mere usurpers, tyrants and what's worse,
To fright the animals and to kill them up[4]
In their assign'd and native dwelling-place.
DUKE S.   And did you leave him in this contemplation?
SEC. LORD.   We did, my lord, weeping and commenting
Upon the sobbing deer.
DUKE S.   Show me the place:
I love to cope[5] him in these sullen fits,
For then he's full of matter.
FIRST LORD.   I'll bring you to him straight.   *[Exeunt.*

SCENE II. *A Room in the Palace.*

Enter DUKE FREDERICK, *with* Lords

DUKE F.   Can it be possible that no man saw them?
It cannot be: some villains of my court
Are of consent and sufferance in this.
FIRST LORD.   I cannot hear of any that did see her.
The ladies, her attendants of her chamber,
Saw her a-bed, and in the morning early
They found the bed untreasured of their mistress.
SEC. LORD.   My lord, the roynish[1] clown, at whom so oft
Your Grace was wont to laugh, is also missing.
Hisperia, the princess' gentlewoman,
Confesses that she secretly o'erheard

---

[4]*kill . . . up*] Intensive of "kill," *i.e.* exterminate. Cf. Adlington's *Apuleius' Golden Asse,* 1582, fo. 159: "*Killed up* with colde."
[5]*cope*] meet with, encounter. Cf. *Venus and Adonis,* 889: "They all strain courtesy who shall *cope* him first."

[1]*roynish*] scurvy. Cognate forms "roynous" and "roignous," both meaning "coarse," figure in the *Romaunt of the Rose,* ll. 987, 6193. The word seems adapted from the French. Cotgrave's *Fr.-Eng. Dict.* has "rougneux," which is interpreted "scabbie, mangie," and "scuruie." Cf. *Macb.,* I, iii, 6: "*rump-fed ronyon* [mangy creature]."

Your daughter and her cousin much commend
The parts and graces of the wrestler
That did but lately foil the sinewy Charles;
And she believes, wherever they are gone,
That youth is surely in their company.
DUKE F.   Send to his brother; fetch that gallant hither;
If he be absent, bring his brother to me;
I'll make him find him: do this suddenly,
And let not search and inquisition quail[2]
To bring again these foolish runaways.   [*Exeunt.*

SCENE III. *Before Oliver's House.*

Enter ORLANDO *and* ADAM, *meeting*

ORL.   Who's there?
ADAM.   What, my young master? O my gentle master!
O my sweet master! O you memory
Of old Sir Rowland! why, what make you here?
Why are you virtuous? why do people love you?
And wherefore are you gentle, strong and valiant?
Why would you be so fond to overcome
The bonny priser[1] of the humorous Duke?
Your praise is come too swiftly home before you.
Know you not, master, to some kind of men
Their graces serve them but as enemies?
No more do yours: your virtues, gentle master,
Are sanctified and holy traitors to you.
O, what a world is this, when what is comely
Envenoms him that bears it!
ORL.   Why, what's the matter?
ADAM.   O unhappy youth!
Come not within these doors; within this roof
The enemy of all your graces lives:

---

[2]*quail*] grow faint, slacken in effort.

[1]*bonny priser*] strong prizefighter (*i.e.*, contender for a prize). The word *bonny* is the reading of all the Folios, and is doubtless right. The epithet is frequently used in the sense of "strong" as well as in that of "comely." Warburton's widely adopted correction, *boney, i.e.*, "muscular," is unnecessary.

Your brother—no, no brother; yet the son—
Yet not the son, I will not call him son,
Of him I was about to call his father,—
Hath heard your praises, and this night he means
To burn the lodging where you use to lie
And you within it: if he fail of that,
He will have other means to cut you off.
I overheard him and his practices.
This is no place;[2] this house is but a butchery:
Abhor it, fear it, do not enter it.

ORL.   Why, whither, Adam, wouldst thou have me go?

ADAM.   No matter whither, so you come not here.

ORL.   What, wouldst thou have me go and beg my food?
Or with a base and boisterous sword enforce
A thievish living on the common road?
This I must do, or know not what to do:
Yet this I will not do, do how I can;
I rather will subject me to the malice
Of a diverted blood[3] and bloody brother.

ADAM.   But do not so. I have five hundred crowns,
The thrifty hire I saved under your father,
Which I did store to be my foster-nurse
When service should in my old limbs lie lame,
And unregarded age in corners thrown:
Take that, and He that doth the ravens feed,
Yea, providently caters for the sparrow,
Be comfort to my age! Here is the gold;
All this I give you. Let me be your servant:
Though I look old, yet I am strong and lusty;
For in my youth I never did apply
Hot and rebellious liquors in my blood,
Nor did not with unbashful forehead woo
The means of weakness and debility;
Therefore my age is as a lusty winter,
Frosty, but kindly: let me go with you;
I'll do the service of a younger man
In all your business and necessities.

ORL.   O good old man, how well in thee appears
The constant service of the antique world,
When service sweat for duty, not for meed!

---

[2]*This is no place*] Cf. *Lover's Complaint*, 82: "Love made him her *place*, [*i.e.*, her home,
place to dwell in]."
[3]*diverted blood*] blood (or natural affection) turned from the course of nature.

Thou art not for the fashion of these times,
Where none will sweat but for promotion,
And having that do choke their service up
Even with the having: it is not so with thee.
But, poor old man, thou prunest a rotten tree,
That cannot so much as a blossom yield
In lieu of all thy pains and husbandry.
But come thy ways; we'll go along together,
And ere we have thy youthful wages spent,
We'll light upon some settled low content.

ADAM. Master, go on, and I will follow thee,
To the last gasp, with truth and loyalty.
From seventeen[4] years till now almost fourscore
Here lived I, but now live here no more.
At seventeen years many their fortunes seek;
But at fourscore it is too late a week:
Yet fortune cannot recompense me better
Than to die well and not my master's debtor.   [*Exeunt.*

SCENE IV. *The Forest of Arden.*

Enter ROSALIND *for* GANYMEDE, CELIA *for* ALIENA, *and* TOUCHSTONE

ROS. O Jupiter, how weary[1] are my spirits!

TOUCH. I care not for my spirits, if my legs were not weary.

ROS. I could find in my heart to disgrace my man's apparel and to cry
like a woman; but I must comfort the weaker vessel, as doublet
and hose[2] ought to show itself courageous to petticoat: therefore,
courage, good Aliena.

CEL. I pray you, bear with me; I cannot go no further.

TOUCH. For my part, I had rather bear with you than bear you: yet I
should bear no cross,[3] if I did bear you; for I think you have no
money in your purse.

---

[4]*seventeen*] This is Rowe's emendation for the *seventy* of the Folios.

---

[1]*weary*] Theobald's emendation of the *merry* of the Folios.

[2]*doublet and hose*] the chief features of male attire in Shakespeare's day.

[3]*bear no cross*] a quibble on the two meanings of the phrase, viz., "endure hardship" and
"carry a coin," specifically known as a "cross," from the stamp upon it of a cross. Cf. 2
Hen. IV, I, ii, 212–213: "you are too impatient to *bear crosses.*"

Ros.   Well, this is the forest of Arden.

Touch.   Ay, now am I in Arden; the more fool I; when I was at home, I was in a better place: but travellers must be content.

Ros.   Ay, be so, good Touchstone.

Enter Corin *and* Silvius

Look you, who comes here; a young man and an old in solemn talk.

Cor.   That is the way to make her scorn you still.

Sil.   O Corin, that thou knew'st how I do love her!

Cor.   I partly guess; for I have loved ere now.

Sil.   No, Corin, being old, thou canst not guess,
Though in thy youth thou wast as true a lover
As ever sigh'd upon a midnight pillow:
But if thy love were ever like to mine,—
As sure I think did never man love so,—
How many actions most ridiculous
Hast thou been drawn to by thy fantasy?[4]

Cor.   Into a thousand that I have forgotten.

Sil.   O, thou didst then ne'er love so heartily!
If thou remember'st not the slightest folly
That ever love did make thee run into,
Thou hast not loved:
Or if thou hast not sat as I do now,
Wearing thy hearer in thy mistress' praise,
Thou hast not loved:
Or if thou hast not broke from company
Abruptly, as my passion now makes me,
Thou hast not loved.
O Phebe, Phebe, Phebe!   [*Exit.*

Ros.   Alas, poor shepherd! searching of thy wound, I have by hard adventure found mine own.

Touch.   And I mine. I remember, when I was in love I broke my sword upon a stone and bid him take that for coming a-night to Jane Smile: and I remember the kissing of her batlet[5] and the cow's dugs that her pretty chopt[6] hands had milked: and I remember the wooing of a peascod instead of her; from whom I took two cods and, giving her them again, said with weeping tears

---

[4]*fantasy*] Used like the cognate form "fancy" in the sense of affection or love.
[5]*batlet*] Thus the Second and later Folios. The First Folio reads *batler*, which there seems no reason for changing. Neither form is met elsewhere. The reference is to the bat or flat wooden instrument (sometimes called a washing-beetle) with which clothes are beaten by the laundress. Cf. Levins's *Manipulus*, 1570, p. 38: "To *battle* clothes. Excutere."
[6]*chopt*] chapped. Cf. *Sonnet* lxii, 10: "*chopp'd* with tann'd antiquity."

"Wear these for my sake." We that are true lovers run into strange capers; but as all is mortal in nature, so is all nature in love mortal in folly.[7]

ROS.　Thou speakest wiser than thou art ware of.

TOUCH.　Nay, I shall ne'er be ware of mine own wit till I break my shins against it.

ROS.　Jove, Jove! this shepherd's passion
Is much upon my fashion.

TOUCH.　And mine; but it grows something stale with me.

CEL.　I pray you, one of you question yond man
If he for gold will give us any food:
I faint almost to death.

TOUCH.　　　　　　　　Holla, you clown!

ROS.　Peace, fool: he's not thy kinsman.

COR.　　　　　　　　　　Who calls?

TOUCH.　Your betters, sir.

COR.　　　　　　　Else are they very wretched.

ROS.　Peace, I say. Good even to you, friend.

COR.　And to you, gentle sir, and to you all.

ROS.　I prithee, shepherd, if that love or gold
Can in this desert place buy entertainment,
Bring us where we may rest ourselves and feed:
Here's a young maid with travel much oppress'd
And faints for succour.

COR.　　　　　　　　Fair sir, I pity her
And wish, for her sake more than for mine own,
My fortunes were more able to relieve her;
But I am shepherd to another man
And do not shear the fleeces that I graze:
My master is of churlish disposition
And little recks to find the way to heaven
By doing deeds of hospitality:
Besides, his cote, his flocks and bounds of feed
Are now on sale, and at our sheepcote now,
By reason of his absence, there is nothing
That you will feed on; but what is, come see,
And in my voice[8] most welcome shall you be.

ROS.　What is he that shall buy his flock and pasture?

COR.　That young swain that you saw here but erewhile,
That little cares for buying any thing.

ROS.　I pray thee, if it stand with honesty,

---

[7]*mortal in folly*] "Mortal" is here a slang intensitive meaning "excessive," "extravagant," with the implied suggestion that folly deals death to love.

[8]*in my voice*] as far as my voice or vote has power to bid you welcome.

Buy thou the cottage, pasture and the flock,
And thou shalt have to pay for it of us.
CEL.   And we will mend thy wages. I like this place,
And willingly could waste my time in it.
COR.   Assuredly the thing is to be sold:
Go with me: if you like upon report
The soil, the profit and this kind of life,
I will your very faithful feeder[9] be
And buy it with your gold right suddenly.   [*Exeunt.*

SCENE V. *The Forest.*

Enter AMIENS, JAQUES, *and others*

SONG

AMI.   Under the greenwood tree
                Who loves to lie with me,
                And turn[1] his merry note
                Unto the sweet bird's throat,
        Come hither, come hither, come hither:
                Here shall he see
                No enemy
        But winter and rough weather.

JAQ.   More, more, I prithee, more.
AMI.   It will make you melancholy, Monsieur Jaques.
JAQ.   I thank it. More, I prithee, more. I can suck melancholy out of
a song, as a weasel sucks eggs. More, I prithee, more.
AMI.   My voice is ragged: I know I cannot please you.
JAQ.   I do not desire you to please me; I do desire you to sing. Come,
more; another stanzo:[2] call you 'em stanzos?
AMI.   What you will, Monsieur Jaques.

---

[9]*feeder*] This word in the sense of "servant" is not uncommon, and various suggested
changes are unnecessary.

[1]*turn*] This is the reading of the Folios, and the word clearly means "adapt." Cf. Hall's
Satires, VI, i: "Martiall *turns* his merry note." Rowe's widely accepted emendation,
tunes, may be rejected.
[2]*stanzo*] Cotgrave, *Fr.-Eng. Dict.*, gives the form "stanzo" (for stanza) when interpret-
ing the French "stance." In *L. L. L.*, IV, ii, 99, "stanze" is read in the original editions,—the First Folio and First Quarto,—and "stanza" in the later Folios. There is an
obvious uncertainty as to the right form.

JAQ.   Nay, I care not for their names; they owe me nothing.[3] Will you
sing?

AMI.   More at your request than to please myself.

JAQ.   Well then, if ever I thank any man, I'll thank you; but that they
call compliment is like the encounter of two dog-apes, and when
a man thanks me heartily, methinks I have given him a penny and
he renders me the beggarly thanks. Come, sing; and you that will
not, hold your tongues.

AMI.   Well, I'll end the song. Sirs, cover[4] the while; the Duke will
drink under this tree. He hath been all this day to look you.

JAQ.   And I have been all this day to avoid him. He is too disputable
for my company: I think of as many matters as he; but I give
heaven thanks, and make no boast of them. Come, warble, come.

SONG

        Who doth ambition shun,   [*All together here.*
        And loves to live i' the sun,
        Seeking the food he eats,
        And pleased with what he gets,
Come hither, come hither, come hither:
          Here shall he see
          No enemy
But winter and rough weather.

JAQ.   I'll give you a verse to this note, that I made yesterday in despite
of my invention.

AMI.   And I'll sing it.

JAQ.   Thus it goes:—

            If it do come to pass
            That any man turn ass,
            Leaving his wealth and ease
            A stubborn will to please,
        Ducdame, ducdame, ducdame:[5]
            Here shall he see
            Gross fools as he,
        And if he will come to me.

[3]*names . . . owe me nothing*] an allusion to the use of the Latin "nomina" in the common sense of "details of debt." Cooper's *Thesaurus*, 1573, defines "Nomina" as "the
names of debtes owen."

[4]*cover*] lay the cloth.

[5]*Ducdame*] In all probability a nonsensical parody of the conventional burden of an
unidentified popular song. Cf. in *All's Well*, I, iii, 69, the clown's senseless sing-song
"Fond done, done fond" in his ditty of Helen of Greece. Attempts have been made to
connect "ducdame" with like-sounding words in Latin, Italian, French, Gaelic, Welsh,
Greek, and Romany.

AMI.   What's that "ducdame"?

JAQ.   'T is a Greek invocation, to call fools into a circle. I'll go sleep, if I can; if I cannot, I'll rail against all the first-born of Egypt.[6]

AMI.   And I'll go seek the Duke: his banquet is prepared.

[Exeunt severally.

SCENE VI. *The Forest.*

Enter ORLANDO *and* ADAM

ADAM.   Dear master, I can go no further; O, I die for food! Here lie I down, and measure out my grave. Farewell, kind master.

ORL.   Why, how now, Adam! no greater heart in thee? Live a little; comfort a little; cheer thyself a little. If this uncouth forest yield any thing savage, I will either be food for it or bring it for food to thee. Thy conceit is nearer death than thy powers. For my sake be comfortable; hold death awhile at the arm's end: I will here be with thee presently; and if I bring thee not something to eat, I will give thee leave to die: but if thou diest before I come, thou art a mocker of my labour. Well said! thou lookest cheerly, and I'll be with thee quickly. Yet thou liest in the bleak air: come, I will bear thee to some shelter; and thou shalt not die for lack of a dinner, if there live any thing in this desert. Cheerly, good Adam!   *[Exeunt.*

SCENE VII. *The Forest.*

A table set out. Enter DUKE SENIOR, AMIENS, *and* Lords *like outlaws*

DUKE S.   I think he be transform'd into a beast;
For I can no where find him like a man.

FIRST LORD.   My lord, he is but even now gone hence:
Here was he merry, hearing of a song.

---

[6]*the first-born of Egypt*] high-born persons.

DUKE S.   If he, compact of jars, grow musical,
  We shall have shortly discord in the spheres.[1]
  Go, seek him: tell him I would speak with him.

Enter JAQUES

FIRST LORD.   He saves my labour by his own approach.
DUKE S.   Why, how now, monsieur! what a life is this,
  That your poor friends must woo your company?
  What, you look merrily!
JAQ.   A fool, a fool! I met a fool i' the forest,
  A motley[2] fool; a miserable world!
  As I do live by food, I met a fool;
  Who laid him down and bask'd him in the sun,
  And rail'd on Lady Fortune in good terms,
  In good set terms, and yet a motley fool.
  "Good morrow, fool," quoth I. "No, sir," quoth he,
  "Call me not fool till heaven hath sent me fortune:"
  And then he drew a dial from his poke,[3]
  And, looking on it with lack-lustre eye,
  Says very wisely, "It is ten o'clock:
  Thus we may see," quoth he, "how the world wags:
  'T is but an hour ago since it was nine;
  And after one hour more 't will be eleven;
  And so, from hour to hour, we ripe and ripe,
  And then, from hour to hour, we rot and rot;
  And thereby hangs a tale." When I did hear
  The motley fool thus moral[4] on the time,
  My lungs began to crow like chanticleer,
  That fools should be so deep-contemplative;
  And I did laugh sans intermission

---

[1]*spheres*] The common belief in the music of the spheres is well illustrated in *Merch. of Ven.*, V, i, 60–61: "There's not the smallest orb which thou behold'st But in his motion like an angel sings."

[2]*motley*] a reference to the conventional parti-coloured or patchwork dress of the professional fool. "Mottled" would be the modern expression. A species of variegated cloth seems to have borne in the trade the name of "motley." Cf. line 34, *infra*, "*Motley's* the only wear," and 43, "a *motley* coat."

[3]*dial from his poke*] It was common among the lower orders to carry in the "poke" or pocket a sundial in the form of a metal ring about two inches in diameter, which was so marked and contrived that sunlight falling upon it indicated the hour of day. A specimen of a pocket dial of the Elizabethan period is preserved in the Museum at Shakespeare's birthplace, Stratford-upon-Avon.

[4]*moral*] Cf. II, i, 44, *supra*, "*moralize* this spectacle." There seems little doubt that "moral on" is a verb meaning "moralize on." The suggestion that "moral" is here used adjectivally offers an awkward construction.

An hour by his dial. O noble fool!
A worthy fool! Motley's the only wear.
DUKE S.   What fool is this?
JAQ.   O worthy fool! One that hath been a courtier,
And says, if ladies be but young and fair,
They have the gift to know it: and in his brain,
Which is as dry as the remainder biscuit
After a voyage, he hath strange places cramm'd[5]
With observation, the which he vents
In mangled forms. O that I were a fool!
I am ambitious for a motley coat.
DUKE S.   Thou shalt have one.
JAQ.   It is my only suit;[6]
Provided that you weed your better judgements
Of all opinion that grows rank in them
That I am wise. I must have liberty
Withal, as large a charter as the wind,[7]
To blow on whom I please; for so fools have;
And they that are most galled with my folly,
They most must laugh. And why, sir, must they so?
The "why" is plain as way to parish church:
He that a fool doth very wisely hit
Doth very foolishly, although he smart,
Not to seem senseless of the bob:[8] if not,
The wise man's folly is anatomized
Even by the squandering glances[9] of the fool.
Invest me in my motley; give me leave
To speak my mind, and I will through and through
Cleanse the foul body of the infected world,
If they will patiently receive my medicine.
DUKE S.   Fie on thee! I can tell what thou wouldst do.
JAQ.   What, for a counter,[10] would I do but good?
DUKE S.   Most mischievous foul sin, in chiding sin:

---

[5]*he hath strange places cramm'd*] he hath collected from observation or study a mass of
strange topics, allusions, passages from books. Cf. the use of the Latin word "loci" and
the Greek "τόποι."
[6]*my only suit*] a quibble on the two meanings of the word "petition" and "dress."
[7]*as large a charter as the wind*] Cf. *Hen. V*, I, i, 48: "The *air*, a *charter'd libertine*, is still."
[8]*Not to . . . bob*] The Folios omit the words *not to*, which Theobald first supplied. They
are necessary to the sense. The general meaning is that the wise man, though he may
smart under a fool's taunt, ought to ignore the "bob" or rap of a fool's comment.
[9]*squandering glances*] random shots.
[10]*counter*] a thing of no value; a metal disc, of no intrinsic value, used in making
calculations.

For thou thyself hast been a libertine,
As sensual as the brutish sting[11] itself;
And all the embossed sores and headed evils,
That thou with license of free foot[12] hast caught,
Wouldst thou disgorge into the general world.

JAQ.   Why, who cries out on pride,
That can therein tax any private party?
Doth it not flow as hugely as the sea,
Till that the weary very means do ebb?[13]
What woman in the city do I name,
When that I say the city-woman bears
The cost of princes on unworthy shoulders?
Who can come in and say that I mean her,
When such a one as she such is her neighbour?
Or what is he of basest function,
That says his bravery is not on my cost,
Thinking that I mean him, but therein suits
His folly to the mettle of my speech?[14]
There then; how then? what then? Let me see wherein
My tongue hath wrong'd him: if it do him right,
Then he hath wrong'd himself; if he be free,
Why then my taxing like a wild-goose flies,
Unclaim'd of any man. But who comes here?

Enter ORLANDO, *with his sword drawn*

ORL.   Forbear, and eat no more.
JAQ.   Why, I have eat none yet.
ORL.   Nor shalt not, till necessity be served.
JAQ.   Of what kind should this cock come of?
DUKE S.   Art thou thus bolden'd, man, by thy distress?
Or else a rude despiser of good manners,
That in civility thou seem'st so empty?
ORL.   You touch'd my vein at first: the thorny point
Of bare distress hath ta'en from me the show

---

[11]*brutish sting*] animal impulse.
[12]*with license of free foot*] gadding about with no restraint.
[13]*Till . . . ebb*] This is the original reading. It means that pride flows on like the tidal sea till its "very means," or sustaining forces, becoming weary or exhausted, ebb or decay. Singer's emendation, *the wearer's very means,* is not happy.
[14]*Or what . . . speech?*] The general meaning is that one finds men in the lowest position in life taking a foolish pride in showy apparel who, if they hear a censorious observer denounce the vanity of spending money on dress, retort that the critic does not pay for what they wear; the critic's censure is intended to have no particular or personal application, but such a reply is a safe sign that the cap fits.

    Of smooth civility: yet am I inland[15] bred
    And know some nurture. But forbear, I say:
    He dies that touches any of this fruit
    Till I and my affairs are answered.
JAQ.   An you will not be answered with reason, I must die.
DUKE S.   What would you have? Your gentleness shall force,
    More than your force move us to gentleness.
ORL.   I almost die for food; and let me have it.
DUKE S.   Sit down and feed, and welcome to our table.
ORL.   Speak you so gently? Pardon me, I pray you:
    I thought that all things had been savage here;
    And therefore put I on the countenance
    Of stern commandment. But whate'er you are
    That in this desert inaccessible,
    Under the shade of melancholy boughs,
    Lose and neglect the creeping hours of time;
    If ever you have look'd on better days,
    If ever been where bells have knoll'd to church,
    If ever sat at any good man's feast,
    If ever from your eyelids wiped a tear
    And know what 't is to pity and be pitied,
    Let gentleness my strong enforcement be:
    In the which hope I blush, and hide my sword.
DUKE S.   True is it that we have seen better days,
    And have with holy bell been knoll'd to church,
    And sat at good men's feasts, and wiped our eyes
    Of drops that sacred pity hath engender'd:
    And therefore sit you down in gentleness
    And take upon command[16] what help we have
    That to your wanting may be minister'd.
ORL.   Then but forbear your food a little while,
    Whiles, like a doe, I go to find my fawn
    And give it food. There is an old poor man,
    Who after me hath many a weary step
    Limp'd in pure love: till he be first sufficed,
    Oppress'd with two weak evils, age and hunger,
    I will not touch a bit.
DUKE S.   Go find him out,
    And we will nothing waste till you return.
ORL.   I thank ye; and be blest for your good comfort!   [*Exit.*

---

[15]*inland*] civilized, refined, the converse of "outlandish." Cf. III, ii, 322, *infra:* "an *in-land* man."
[16]*upon command*] at your command.

DUKE S.　Thou seest we are not all alone unhappy:
　　This wide and universal theatre
　　Presents more woeful pageants than the scene
　　Wherein we play in.
JAQ.　　　　　　　　　　All the world's a stage,[17]
　　And all the men and women merely players:
　　They have their exits and their entrances;
　　And one man in his time plays many parts,
　　His acts being seven ages. At first the infant,
　　Mewling and puking in the nurse's arms.
　　Then the whining school-boy, with his satchel
　　And shining morning face, creeping like snail
　　Unwillingly to school. And then the lover,
　　Sighing like furnace,[18] with a woeful ballad
　　Made to his mistress' eyebrow. Then a soldier,
　　Full of strange oaths, and bearded like the pard,
　　Jealous in honour, sudden and quick in quarrel,
　　Seeking the bubble reputation
　　Even in the cannon's mouth. And then the justice,
　　In fair round belly with good capon[19] lined,
　　With eyes severe and beard of formal cut,
　　Full of wise saws and modern instances;[20]
　　And so he plays his part. The sixth age shifts
　　Into the lean and slipper'd pantaloon,
　　With spectacles on nose and pouch on side,
　　His youthful hose, well saved, a world too wide
　　For his shrunk shank; and his big manly voice,
　　Turning again toward childish treble, pipes
　　And whistles in his sound. Last scene of all,
　　That ends this strange eventful history,
　　Is second childishness and mere oblivion,

---

[17]*All . . . stage*] Cf. *Merch. of Ven.*, I, i, 77–78: "I hold the world but as the world, Gratiano; A stage, where every man must play a part." The comparison of the world to a stage was a commonplace in Greek, Latin, and modern European literature. The Globe Theatre bore the proverbial motto, "Totus mundus agit histrionem." The division of man's life into seven parts or ages, which Shakespeare likens to acts of a play, is found in the Greek writings of the physician Hippocrates and of the late Greek philosopher Proclus, and was generally accepted by philosophers, poets, and artists of the European Renaissance.

[18]*Sighing like furnace*] Cf. *Cymb.*, I, vi, 65–66: "he [*i.e.*, a Frenchman in love] *furnaces* The thick *sighs* from him."

[19]*the justice . . . capon*] Capons formed gifts which suitors were in the habit of offering justices of the peace. Cf. Wither's *Christmas Carol*, lines 41, 42: "Now poor men to the *justices* With *capons* make their arrants [*i.e.*, errands]."

[20]*modern instances*] trite or commonplace maxims or anecdotes.

Sans teeth, sans eyes, sans taste, sans every thing.

Re-enter ORLANDO, *with* ADAM

DUKE S.   Welcome. Set down your venerable burthen,
And let him feed.
ORL.   I thank you most for him.
ADAM.   So had you need:
I scarce can speak to thank you for myself.
DUKE S.   Welcome; fall to: I will not trouble you
As yet, to question you about your fortunes.
Give us some music; and, good cousin, sing.

SONG

AMI.   Blow, blow, thou winter wind,
                         Thou art not so unkind
                              As man's ingratitude;
                         Thy tooth is not so keen,
                         Because thou art not seen,
                              Although thy breath be rude.
                  Heigh-ho! sing, heigh-ho! unto the green holly:
                  Most friendship is feigning, most loving mere folly:
                         Then, heigh-ho, the holly!
                              This life is most jolly.

                         Freeze, freeze, thou bitter sky,
                         That does not bite so nigh
                              As benefits forgot:
                         Though thou the waters warp,
                         Thy sting is not so sharp
                              As friend remember'd not.
                  Heigh-ho! sing, &c.

DUKE S.   If that you were the good Sir Rowland's son,
As you have whisper'd faithfully you were,
And as mine eye doth his effigies[21] witness
Most truly limn'd and living in your face,
Be truly welcome hither: I am the Duke
That loved your father: the residue of your fortune,
Go to my cave and tell me. Good old man,
Thou art right welcome as thy master is.
Support him by the arm. Give me your hand,
And let me all your fortunes understand.   [*Exeunt.*

---

[21]*effigies*] The accent in this word, which must be pronounced trisyllabically, falls on the second syllable.

ACT III.

SCENE I. *A Room in the Palace.*

Enter DUKE FREDERICK, Lords, *and* OLIVER

DUKE FREDERICK.   Not see him since? Sir, sir, that cannot be:
   But were I not the better part made mercy,
   I should not seek an absent argument
   Of my revenge, thou present. But look to it:
   Find out thy brother, wheresoe'er he is;
   Seek him with candle; bring him dead or living
   Within this twelvemonth, or turn thou no more
   To seek a living in our territory:
   Thy lands and all things that thou dost call thine
   Worth seizure do we seize into our hands,
   Till thou canst quit thee by thy brother's mouth
   Of what we think against thee.
OLI.   O that your Highness knew my heart in this!
   I never loved my brother in my life.
DUKE F.   More villain thou. Well, push him out of doors;
   And let my officers of such a nature
   Make an extent upon[1] his house and lands:
   Do this expediently and turn him going.   [*Exeunt.*

---

[1]*Make an extent upon, etc.*] In strict legal phraseology the process of "making an extent," *i.e.*, executing the writ "extendi facias," consisted in appraising the value of property to its full extent as a preliminary to its summary seizure. The process ordinarily followed a sentence of forfeiture of which in the present instance Shakespeare gives no hint. The phrase is very commonly met with in Elizabethan plays in the loose significance, as here, of taking forcible possession of property.

SCENE II. *The Forest.*

Enter ORLANDO, *with a paper*

ORL.   Hang there, my verse, in witness of my love:
     And thou, thrice-crowned queen of night,[1] survey
With thy chaste eye, from thy pale sphere above,
     Thy huntress' name that my full life doth sway.
O Rosalind! these trees shall be my books
     And in their barks my thoughts I'll character;
That every eye which in this forest looks
     Shall see thy virtue witness'd every where.
Run, run, Orlando; carve on every tree
The fair, the chaste and unexpressive[2] she.   [*Exit.*

Enter CORIN *and* TOUCHSTONE

COR.   And how like you this shepherd's life, Master Touchstone?

TOUCH.   Truly, shepherd, in respect of itself, it is a good life; but in respect that it is a shepherd's life, it is naught. In respect that it is solitary, I like it very well; but in respect that it is private, it is a very vile life. Now, in respect it is in the fields, it pleaseth me well; but in respect it is not in the court, it is tedious. As it is a spare life, look you, it fits my humour well; but as there is no more plenty in it, it goes much against my stomach. Hast any philosophy in thee, shepherd?

COR.   No more but that I know the more one sickens the worse at ease he is; and that he that wants money, means and content is without three good friends; that the property of rain is to wet and fire to burn; that good pasture makes fat sheep, and that a great cause of the night is lack of the sun; that he that hath learned no wit by nature nor art may complain of good breeding[3] or comes of a very dull kindred.

---

[1] *thrice-crowned queen of night*] Luna, or the moon, was believed in classical mythology to rule three realms,—earth, heaven, where she was known as "Diana," and the infernal regions, where she was known as "Hecate." Chapman, in his *Hymn to Night* (1594), describes how the goddess with "triple forehead" controls earth, seas, and hell. Cf. *Mids. N. Dr.*, V, i, 391: "the *triple* Hecate's team."

[2] *unexpressive*] inexpressible; a common usage. Cf. Milton's *Lycidas*, 176: "The *unexpressive* nuptial song."

[3] *good breeding*] i.e., the want of good breeding; a common manner of speech in Elizabethan English.

TOUCH. Such a one is a natural philosopher. Wast ever in court, shepherd?

COR. No, truly.

TOUCH. Then thou art damned.

COR. Nay, I hope.

TOUCH. Truly, thou art damned, like an ill-roasted egg all on one side.

COR. For not being at court? Your reason.

TOUCH. Why, if thou never wast at court, thou never sawest good manners; if thou never sawest good manners, then thy manners must be wicked; and wickedness is sin, and sin is damnation. Thou art in a parlous state, shepherd.

COR. Not a whit, Touchstone: those that are good manners at the court are as ridiculous in the country as the behaviour of the country is most mockable at the court. You told me you salute not at the court, but you kiss[4] your hands: that courtesy would be uncleanly, if courtiers were shepherds.

TOUCH. Instance, briefly; come, instance.

COR. Why, we are still handling our ewes, and their fells, you know, are greasy.

TOUCH. Why, do not your courtier's hands sweat? and is not the grease of a mutton as wholesome as the sweat of a man? Shallow, shallow. A better instance, I say; come.

COR. Besides, our hands are hard.

TOUCH. Your lips will feel them the sooner. Shallow again. A more sounder instance, come.

COR. And they are often tarred over with the surgery of our sheep; and would you have us kiss tar? The courtier's hands are perfumed with civet.

TOUCH. Most shallow man! thou worms-meat, in respect of a good piece of flesh indeed! Learn of the wise, and perpend: civet is of a baser birth than tar, the very uncleanly flux of a cat. Mend the instance, shepherd.

COR. You have too courtly a wit for me: I'll rest.

TOUCH. Wilt thou rest damned? God help thee, shallow man! God make incision in thee! thou art raw.[5]

COR. Sir, I am a true labourer: I earn that I eat, get that I wear, owe no man hate, envy no man's happiness, glad of other men's good, content with my harm, and the greatest of my pride is to see my ewes graze and my lambs suck.

---

[4]*but you kiss*] without kissing.

[5]*God make incision . . . raw*] A reference to blood-letting, which was the accepted method of treating diseases alike of mind or body. "Raw" seems used in a double sense of "ignorant" and "suffering from a flesh wound," which requires medical treatment.

TOUCH. That is another simple sin in you, to bring the ewes and the rams together and to offer to get your living by the copulation of cattle; to be bawd to a bell-wether, and to betray a she-lamb of a twelvemonth to a crooked-pated, old, cuckoldly ram, out of all reasonable match. If thou beest not damned for this, the devil himself will have no shepherds; I cannot see else how thou shouldst 'scape.

COR. Here comes young Master Ganymede, my new mistress's brother.

Enter ROSALIND, *with a paper, reading*

ROS.   From the east to western Ind,
     No jewel is like Rosalind.
     Her worth, being mounted on the wind,
     Through all the world bears Rosalind.
     All the pictures fairest lined
     Are but black to Rosalind.
     Let no face be kept in mind
     But the fair of Rosalind.

TOUCH. I'll rhyme you so eight years together, dinners and suppers and sleeping-hours excepted: it is the right butter-women's rank[6] to market.

ROS. Out, fool!

TOUCH. For a taste:

     If a hart do lack a hind,
     Let him seek out Rosalind.
     If the cat will after kind,
     So be sure will Rosalind.
     Winter garments must be lined,
     So must slender Rosalind.
     They that reap must sheaf and bind;
     Then to cart with Rosalind.
     Sweetest nut hath sourest rind,
     Such a nut is Rosalind.
     He that sweetest rose will find,
     Must find love's prick and Rosalind.

[6]*rank*] This, the original reading, has been much questioned, and the numerous suggested substitutes for *rank* include *rate*, *rack*, *canter*, and others. It is clear that the sense required is that of a jog trot or ambling pace, such as characterises butter-women on their way to market. Such a meaning may possibly be deducible from the women's practice of riding or walking in file or *rank*. Cf. Pettie's translation of Guazzo's, *Civil Conversation* (1586): "All the women in the towne runne thether *of a ranke*, as it were in procession." But much is to be said for the emendation *rack*, which was in common use for a horse's jogging method of progression.

This is the very false gallop[7] of verses: why do you infect yourself
with them?

Ros.   Peace, you dull fool! I found them on a tree.

Touch.   Truly, the tree yields bad fruit.

Ros.   I'll graff it with you, and then I shall graff it with a medlar: then
it will be the earliest fruit[8] i' the country; for you'll be rotten ere
you be half ripe, and that's the right virtue of the medlar.

Touch.   You have said; but whether wisely or no, let the forest judge.

Enter CELIA, *with a writing*

Ros.   Peace!
Here comes my sister, reading: stand aside.

CEL. [*reads*]   Why should this a desert be?
                For it is unpeopled? No;
            Tongues I'll hang on every tree,
                That shall civil sayings show:
            Some, how brief the life of man
                Runs his erring pilgrimage,
            That the stretching of a span
                Buckles in his sum of age;
            Some, of violated vows
                'Twixt the souls of friend and friend:
            But upon the fairest boughs,
                Or at every sentence end,
            Will I Rosalinda write,
                Teaching all that read to know
            The quintessence of every sprite
                Heaven would in little[9] show.
            Therefore Heaven Nature charged
                That one body should be fill'd
            With all graces wide-enlarged:
                Nature presently distill'd
            Helen's cheek, but not her heart,
                Cleopatra's majesty,

---

[7]*false gallop*] Cf. Nashe's *Foure Letters*, "I would trot *a false gallop* through the rest of
his ragged *verses*." The term technically means the jerky amble in which the horse puts
the left foot before the right. Shakespeare, in *1 Hen. IV*, III, i, 134–135, likens "minc-
ing poetry" to the "forced gait of a shuffling nag."

[8]*earliest fruit*] The medlar is now one of the latest fruits to ripen. The circumstance that
it rots ere it ripens argues a premature precocity, which may justify Rosalind's quibbling argument.

[9]*in little*] The train of thought has here astrological significance, and "in little" probably refers to the "microcosm, the little world of man," which is a miniature reflection
of the stars. "A picture *in little*," as in *Hamlet*, II, ii, 362, was a common synonym for
a miniature painting. But there is no such reference here.

Atalanta's better part,[10]
Sad Lucretia's modesty.
Thus Rosalind of many parts
By heavenly synod was devised;
Of many faces, eyes and hearts,
To have the touches dearest prized.
Heaven would that she these gifts should have,
And I to live and die her slave.

Ros.   O most gentle pulpiter![11] what tedious homily of love have you
wearied your parishioners withal, and never cried "Have patience,
good people"!

Cel.   How now! back, friends! Shepherd, go off a little. Go with him,
sirrah.

Touch.   Come, shepherd, let us make an honourable retreat; though
not with bag and baggage, yet with scrip and scrippage.

[*Exeunt* Corin *and* Touchstone.

Cel.   Didst thou hear these verses?

Ros.   O, yes, I heard them all, and more too; for some of them had in
them more feet than the verses would bear.

Cel.   That's no matter: the feet might bear the verses.

Ros.   Ay, but the feet were lame and could not bear themselves without the verse and therefore stood lamely in the verse.

Cel.   But didst thou hear without wondering how thy name should be
hanged and carved upon these trees?

Ros.   I was seven of the nine days out of the wonder before you came;
for look here what I found on a palm-tree. I was never so be-
rhymed since Pythagoras' time, that I was an Irish rat,[12] which I
can hardly remember.

Cel.   Trow you who hath done this?

Ros.   Is it a man?

---

[10]*Atalanta's better part*] Ovid declares himself unable to decide whether Atalanta more
excelled in swiftness of foot or in beauty of face (*Met.*, X, 562–563). In line 260, *infra*,
reference is made to "Atalanta's heels," the first of her two distinctive characteristics.
At this place Shakespeare probably had in mind the charm of feature which Ovid puts
to her credit.

[11]*pulpiter*] *i.e.*, preacher. This is Spedding's ingenious substitute for *Jupiter* of the Folios.
But Rosalind has already made one appeal to Jupiter (II, iv, 1), and has twice called
on Jove (II, iv, 56), while she makes a passing reference to the god at III, ii, 221, *infra*.
Irrelevant use of these expletives of adjuration seems in keeping with her character,
and the old reading may possibly be right.

[12]*be-rhymed . . . Irish rat*] Cf. Jonson's *Poetaster*, Dialogue to the Reader, 150–151:
"*Rime* 'hem to death, as they doe *Irish rats* In drumming tunes." The superstitious belief that rats can be rhymed to death seems to be cherished by the peasantry of France
as well as of Ireland.

CEL. And a chain, that you once wore, about his neck. Change you colour?

ROS. I prithee, who?

CEL. O Lord, Lord! it is a hard matter for friends to meet; but mountains may be removed with earthquakes and so encounter.

ROS. Nay, but who is it?

CEL. Is it possible?

ROS. Nay, I prithee now with most petitionary vehemence, tell me who it is.

CEL. O wonderful, wonderful, and most wonderful wonderful! and yet again wonderful, and after that, out of all hooping![13]

ROS. Good my complexion![14] dost thou think, though I am caparisoned like a man, I have a doublet and hose in my disposition? One inch of delay more is a South-sea of discovery;[15] I prithee, tell me who is it quickly, and speak apace. I would thou couldst stammer, that thou mightst pour this concealed man out of thy mouth, as wine comes out of a narrow-mouthed bottle, either too much at once, or none at all. I prithee, take the cork out of thy mouth that I may drink thy tidings.

CEL. So you may put a man in your belly.

ROS. Is he of God's making?[16] What manner of man? Is his head worth a hat? or his chin worth a beard?

CEL. Nay, he hath but a little beard.

ROS. Why, God will send more, if the man will be thankful: let me stay the growth of his beard, if thou delay me not the knowledge of his chin.

CEL. It is young Orlando, that tripped up the wrestler's heels and your heart both in an instant.

ROS. Nay, but the devil take mocking: speak sad brow and true maid.[17]

CEL. I' faith, coz, 't is he.

---

[13]*out of all hooping!*] beyond all the limits of wonder which shouting can adequately express.

[14]*Good my complexion!*] This exclamation seems a nervous and involuntary appeal to Rosalind's feminine tell-tale complexion. The inversion of the epithet "good," which is very common in Elizabethan English, somewhat obscures the meaning, which amounts in effect to nothing more than an ebullition of anxiety lest her girl's face shall betray her.

[15]*One inch of delay more is a South-sea of discovery*] The slightest delay in satisfying my curiosity will expose me to the uncertainties and perplexities of an exploring voyage in some great unknown ocean like the unexplored South-sea or Pacific Ocean.

[16]*of God's making?*] The implied alternative is "a man of his tailor's making." Cf. *Lear*, II, ii, 50: "nature disclaims in thee: a tailor made thee."

[17]*speak . . . maid*] speak in all seriousness and truth. Cf. for the construction 258, *infra*, "I *answer you right painted cloth*," and K. *John*, II, i, 462: "He *speaks plain cannon fire*, and smoke and bounce."

Ros.   Orlando?
Cel.   Orlando.
Ros.   Alas the day! what shall I do with my doublet and hose? What
did he when thou sawest him? What said he? How looked he?
Wherein went he?[18] What makes he here? Did he ask for me?
Where remains he? How parted he with thee? and when shalt
thou see him again? Answer me in one word.
Cel.   You must borrow me Gargantua's mouth[19] first: 't is a word too
great for any mouth of this age's size. To say ay and no to these par-
ticulars is more than to answer in a catechism.
Ros.   But doth he know that I am in this forest and in man's apparel?
Looks he as freshly as he did the day he wrestled?
Cel.   It is as easy to count atomies[20] as to resolve the propositions of a
lover; but take a taste of my finding him, and relish it with good
observance. I found him under a tree, like a dropped acorn.
Ros.   It may well be called Jove's tree,[21] when it drops forth such fruit.
Cel.   Give me audience, good madam.
Ros.   Proceed.
Cel.   There lay he, stretched along, like a wounded knight.
Ros.   Though it be pity to see such a sight, it well becomes the
ground.
Cel.   Cry "holla"[22] to thy tongue, I prithee; it curvets unseasonably.
He was furnished like a hunter.
Ros.   O, ominous! he comes to kill my heart.[23]
Cel.   I would sing my song without a burden: thou bringest me out of
tune.
Ros.   Do you not know I am a woman? when I think, I must speak.
Sweet, say on.
Cel.   You bring me out. Soft! comes he not here?

Enter ORLANDO *and* JAQUES

Ros.   'T is he: slink by, and note him.

---

[18]*Wherein went he?*] How did he go dressed?

[19]*Gargantua's mouth*] Gargantua, Rabelais' giant, swallows five pilgrims with their
staves in a salad (Bk. I, ch. 38). Cf. Cotgrave's *Fr.-Engl. Dict.*, "Gargantua. Great
throat, Rab."

[20]*atomies*] The Third and Fourth Folios read *atomes*, which Rowe changed to *atoms*.
"Atomies" is used again in III, v, 13, *infra*.

[21]*Jove's tree*] Latin poets call the oak "Jove's tree." Shakespeare here seems to have bor-
rowed direct from Golding's Ovid, *Met.*, I, 106: "The *acornes dropt* on ground from
Joves brode tree in feelde."

[22]*"holla"*] stop! Cf. *Venus and Adonis*, 283–284: "What recketh he the rider's angry stir,
His flattering '*Holla*,' or his 'Stand, I say'?"

[23]*heart*] A common quibble between "heart" and "hart."

JAQ. I thank you for your company; but, good faith, I had as lief have been myself alone.

ORL. And so had I; but yet, for fashion sake,
I thank you too for your society.

JAQ. God buy you:[24] let's meet as little as we can.

ORL. I do desire we may be better strangers.

JAQ. I pray you, mar no more trees with writing love-songs in their barks.

ORL. I pray you, mar no moe[25] of my verses with reading them ill-favouredly.

JAQ. Rosalind is your love's name?

ORL. Yes, just.

JAQ. I do not like her name.

ORL. There was no thought of pleasing you when she was christened.

JAQ. What stature is she of?

ORL. Just as high as my heart.

JAQ. You are full of pretty answers. Have you not been acquainted with goldsmiths' wives, and conned them out of rings?[26]

ORL. Not so; but I answer you right painted cloth,[27] from whence you have studied your questions.

JAQ. You have a nimble wit: I think 't was made of Atalanta's heels.[28] Will you sit down with me? and we two will rail against our mistress the world, and all our misery.

ORL. I will chide no breather[29] in the world but myself, against whom I know most faults.

JAQ. The worst fault you have is to be in love.

ORL. 'T is a fault I will not change for your best virtue. I am weary of you.

JAQ. By my troth, I was seeking for a fool when I found you.

ORL. He is drowned in the brook: look but in, and you shall see him.

JAQ. There I shall see mine own figure.

ORL. Which I take to be either a fool or a cipher.

[24]*God buy you*] *buy* is the reading of the Folios. It is equivalent to "God b' wi' you," *i.e.*, "God be with you." Jaques repeats it, IV, i, 28, *infra*, and Touchstone in V, iv, 37.

[25]*moe*] This is the reading of the First Folio, which the later Folios change to the modern *more*.

[26]*goldsmiths' . . . rings*] Goldsmiths dealt largely at the time in rings on which were inscribed posies or mottoes.

[27]*right painted cloth*] Painted cloth was the term applied to cheap tapestries, on which tales from scripture or from popular literature were represented together with moral maxims or mottoes. Labels bearing brief speeches were sometimes attached to the mouths of the figures. Such speeches Orlando charges Jaques with studying. Cf., for a similar construction, line 199, *supra*, "*speak sad brow* and true maid."

[28]*Atalanta's heels*] Cf. note on line 137, *supra* (see footnote 10).

[29]*breather*] Cf. *Sonnet* lxxxi, 12: "When all the *breathers of this world* are dead.",

JAQ. I'll tarry no longer with you: farewell, good Signior Love.

ORL. I am glad of your departure: adieu, good Monsieur Melancholy.

[*Exit* JAQUES.

ROS. [*Aside to* CELIA] I will speak to him like a saucy lackey, and under that habit play the knave with him. Do you hear, forester?

ORL. Very well: what would you?

ROS. I pray you, what is 't o'clock?

ORL. You should ask me what time o' day: there's no clock in the forest.

ROS. Then there is no true lover in the forest; else sighing every minute and groaning every hour would detect the lazy foot of Time as well as a clock.

ORL. And why not the swift foot of Time? had not that been as proper?

ROS. By no means, sir: Time travels in divers paces with divers persons. I'll tell you who Time ambles withal, who Time trots withal, who Time gallops withal and who he stands still withal.

ORL. I prithee, who doth he trot withal?

ROS. Marry, he trots hard with a young maid between the contract of her marriage and the day it is solemnized: if the interim be but a se'nnight, Time's pace is so hard that it seems the length of seven year.

ORL. Who ambles Time withal?

ROS. With a priest that lacks Latin, and a rich man that hath not the gout; for the one sleeps easily because he cannot study, and the other lives merrily because he feels no pain; the one lacking the burden of lean and wasteful learning, the other knowing no burden of heavy tedious penury: these Time ambles withal.

ORL. Who doth he gallop withal?

ROS. With a thief to the gallows; for though he go as softly as foot can fall, he thinks himself too soon there.

ORL. Who stays it still withal?

ROS. With lawyers in the vacation; for they sleep between term and term and then they perceive not how Time moves.

ORL. Where dwell you, pretty youth?

ROS. With this shepherdess, my sister: here in the skirts of the forest, like fringe upon a petticoat.

ORL. Are you native of this place?

ROS. As the cony that you see dwell where she is kindled.

ORL. Your accent is something finer than you could purchase in so removed a dwelling.

ROS. I have been told so of many: but indeed an old religious uncle of mine taught me to speak, who was in his youth an inland[30] man; one that knew courtship too well, for there he fell in love. I have heard him read many lectures against it, and I thank God I am not a woman, to be touched with so many giddy offences as he hath generally taxed their whole sex withal.

ORL.   Can you remember any of the principal evils that he laid to the charge of women?

ROS.   There were none principal; they were all like one another as half-pence are, every one fault seeming monstrous till his fellow-fault came to match it.

ORL.   I prithee, recount some of them.

ROS.   No, I will not cast away my physic but on those that are sick. There is a man haunts the forest, that abuses our young plants with carving Rosalind on their barks; hangs odes upon hawthorns and elegies on brambles; all, forsooth, deifying the name of Rosalind: if I could meet that fancy-monger, I would give him some good counsel, for he seems to have the quotidian of love[31] upon him.

ORL.   I am he that is so love-shaked: I pray you, tell me your remedy.

ROS.   There is none of my uncle's marks upon you: he taught me how to know a man in love; in which cage[32] of rushes I am sure you are not prisoner.

ORL.   What were his marks?

ROS.   A lean cheek, which you have not; a blue eye[33] and sunken, which you have not; an unquestionable[34] spirit, which you have not; a beard neglected, which you have not; but I pardon you for that, for simply your having in beard is a younger brother's revenue: then your hose should be ungartered, your bonnet unbanded,[35] your sleeve unbuttoned, your shoe untied and every thing about you demonstrating a careless desolation; but you are no such man; you are rather point-device in your accoutrements, as loving yourself than seeming the lover of any other.

---

[30]*inland*] refined. Cf. II, vii, 96, *supra*, "*inland* bred."

[31]*fancy-monger . . . quotidian of love*] Cf. Lyly's *Euphues* (p. 66): "If euer she haue been taken with the feuer of *fancie* [*i.e.*, love], she will help his ague, who by his *quotidian fit* [*i.e.*, daily recurring paroxysm of fever] is conuerted into phrensie."

[32]*cage*] often used for "prison." Rosalind mockingly suggests that Orlando's prison has rushes for bars, and is no serious impediment.

[33]*blue eye*] eye with a dark circle around it. Cf. *Tempest*, I, ii, 269: "*blue-eyed* hag."

[34]*unquestionable*] averse to conversation. Cf. *Hamlet*, I, iv, 43, "Thou comest in such a *questionable* shape," where "questionable" means "inciting to conversation," "willing to be conversed with."

[35]*bonnet unbanded*] Hats without hatbands were at the time regarded as signs of slovenliness in dress.

ORL. Fair youth, I would I could make thee believe I love.

ROS. Me believe it! you may as soon make her that you love believe it; which, I warrant, she is apter to do than to confess she does: that is one of the points in the which women still give the lie to their consciences. But, in good sooth, are you he that hangs the verses on the trees, wherein Rosalind is so admired?

ORL. I swear to thee, youth, by the white hand of Rosalind, I am that he, that unfortunate he.

ROS. But are you so much in love as your rhymes speak?

ORL. Neither rhyme nor reason can express how much.

ROS. Love is merely a madness; and, I tell you, deserves as well a dark house and a whip as madmen do:[36] and the reason why they are not so punished and cured is, that the lunacy is so ordinary that the whippers are in love too. Yet I profess curing it by counsel.

ORL. Did you ever cure any so?

ROS. Yes, one, and in this manner. He was to imagine me his love, his mistress; and I set him every day to woo me: at which time would I, being but a moonish youth, grieve, be effeminate, changeable, longing and liking; proud, fantastical, apish, shallow, inconstant, full of tears, full of smiles; for every passion something and for no passion truly any thing, as boys and women are for the most part cattle of this colour: would now like him, now loathe him; then entertain him, then forswear him; now weep for him, then spit at him; that I drave my suitor from his mad humour of love to a living[37] humour of madness; which was, to forswear the full stream of the world and to live in a nook merely monastic. And thus I cured him; and this way will I take upon me to wash your liver as clean as a sound sheep's heart, that there shall not be one spot of love in 't.

ORL. I would not be cured, youth.

ROS. I would cure you, if you would but call me Rosalind and come every day to my cote and woo me.

ORL. Now, by the faith of my love, I will: tell me where it is.

ROS. Go with me to it and I'll show it you: and by the way you shall tell me where in the forest you live. Will you go?

ORL. With all my heart, good youth.

ROS. Nay, you must call me Rosalind. Come, sister, will you go?

                    [*Exeunt.*

---

[36] *a dark house and a whip as madmen do*] this was the ordinary treatment of lunatics at the time. Cf. Malvolio's experience in *Tw. Night*, V, i.

[37] *mad . . . living*] unreasoning . . . real or actual.

SCENE III. *The Forest.*

Enter TOUCHSTONE *and* AUDREY; JAQUES *behind*

TOUCH. Come apace, good Audrey: I will fetch up your goats, Audrey. And how, Audrey? am I the man yet? doth my simple feature content you?

AUD. Your features![1] Lord warrant us! what features?

TOUCH. I am here with thee and thy goats, as the most capricious poet, honest Ovid, was among the Goths.[2]

JAQ. [*Aside*] O knowledge ill-inhabited, worse than Jove in a thatched house![3]

TOUCH. When a man's verses cannot be understood, nor a man's good wit seconded with the forward child, understanding, it strikes a man more dead than a great reckoning in a little room.[4] Truly, I would the gods had made thee poetical.

AUD. I do not know what "poetical" is: is it honest in deed and word? is it a true thing?

TOUCH. No, truly; for the truest poetry is the most feigning; and lovers are given to poetry, and what they swear in poetry may be said as lovers they do feign.

AUD. Do you wish then that the gods had made me poetical?

TOUCH. I do, truly; for thou swearest to me thou art honest: now, if thou wert a poet, I might have some hope thou didst feign.

AUD. Would you not have me honest?

TOUCH. No, truly, unless thou wert hard-favoured; for honesty coupled to beauty is to have honey a sauce to sugar.

JAQ. [*Aside*] A material fool!

AUD. Well, I am not fair; and therefore I pray the gods make me honest.

---

[1]*feature . . . features?*] This word was used in the three senses of (1) comeliness, (2) the build of the body, and (3) any part of the face. Touchstone apparently employs it in the first sense, and Audrey in the last. It is possible that there is an implied pun in Audrey's "what features?" on the word "faitor," *i.e.*, a villain, with which "feature" might easily be confused in pronunciation.

[2]*capricious . . . Goths*] "Capricious" is of course from the Latin "caper," a goat. "Goths" was so pronounced as to make the pun on "goats" quite clear. As a matter of history, Ovid was banished to the land of the Getae.

[3]*Jove . . . house*] The reference is to the thatched cottage of the peasants Philemon and Baucis, who entertained Jove unawares, according to Ovid, *Metam.*, VIII, 630, *seq.* There is another allusion to the story in *Much Ado*, II, i, 82–83: (D. Pedro.) "My visor is *Philemon's roof*; within the house is *Jove.* (Hero.) Why then, your visor should be *thatched.*"

[4]*great reckoning . . . room*] a heavy bill for a narrow accommodation.

TOUCH.   Truly, and to cast away honesty upon a foul slut were to put
   good meat into an unclean dish.

AUD.   I am not a slut, though I thank the gods I am foul.[5]

TOUCH.   Well, praised be the gods for thy foulness! sluttishness may
   come hereafter. But be it as it may be, I will marry thee, and to
   that end I have been with Sir Oliver Martext the vicar of the next
   village, who hath promised to meet me in this place of the forest
   and to couple us.

JAQ.   [*Aside*]   I would fain see this meeting.

AUD.   Well, the gods give us joy!

TOUCH.   Amen. A man may, if he were of a fearful heart, stagger in
   this attempt; for here we have no temple but the wood, no assembly but horn-beasts. But what though? Courage! As horns are odi-
   ous, they are necessary. It is said, "many a man knows no end of
   his goods:" right; many a man has good horns, and knows no end
   of them. Well, that is the dowry of his wife; 't is none of his own
   getting. Horns?—even so:—poor men alone?[6] No, no; the noblest
   deer hath them as huge as the rascal. Is the single man therefore
   blessed? No: as a walled town is more worthier than a village, so is
   the forehead of a married man more honourable than the bare
   brow of a bachelor; and by how much defence[7] is better than no
   skill, by so much is a horn more precious than to want. Here
   comes Sir Oliver.

Enter SIR OLIVER MARTEXT

   Sir Oliver Martext, you are well met: will you dispatch us here
   under this tree, or shall we go with you to your chapel?

SIR OLI.   Is there none here to give the woman?

TOUCH.   I will not take her on gift of any man.

SIR OLI.   Truly, she must be given, or the marriage is not lawful.

JAQ.   Proceed, proceed: I'll give her.

TOUCH.   Good even, good Master What-ye-call 't: how do you, sir?
   You are very well met: God 'ild[8] you for your last company:
   I am very glad to see you: even a toy in hand here, sir: nay, pray
   be covered.

JAQ.   Will you be married, motley?

---

[5]*foul*] the word meant "plain" or "homely," more frequently than "base" or "dirty." It
   was the ordinary antithesis of "fair."

[6]*Horns? . . . alone?*] The Folios read: *hornes, euen so poore men alone.* Theobald introduced the punctuation adopted in the text, which makes the passage intelligible.

[7]*defence*] art of fencing. Cf. *Hamlet*, IV, vii, 97: "art and exercise in your *defence*."

[8]*God 'ild*] God yield or reward you. The phrase is repeated by Touchstone, V, iv, 53,
   infra. Cf. *Ant. and Cleop.*, IV, ii, 33: "And the gods *yield* you for 't."

TOUCH.   As the ox hath his bow,[9] sir, the horse his curb and the fal-
con her bells, so man hath his desires; and as pigeons bill, so wedlock would be nibbling.

JAQ.   And will you, being a man of your breeding, be married under a
bush like a beggar? Get you to church, and have a good priest that
can tell you what marriage is: this fellow will but join you together
as they join wainscot; then one of you will prove a shrunk panel,
and like green timber warp, warp.

TOUCH. [*Aside*]   I am not in the mind but I were better to be married
of him than of another: for he is not like to marry me well; and not
being well married, it will be a good excuse for me hereafter to
leave my wife.

JAQ.   Go thou with me, and let me counsel thee.

TOUCH.   Come, sweet Audrey:
We must be married, or we must live in bawdry.
Farewell, good Master Oliver: not,—

> O sweet Oliver,[10]
> O brave Oliver,
> Leave me not behind thee:

but,—

> Wind away,[11]
> Begone, I say,
> I will not to wedding with thee.

> [*Exeunt* JAQUES, TOUCHSTONE, *and* AUDREY.

SIR OLI.   'T is no matter: ne'er a fantastical knave of them all shall
flout me out of my calling.   [*Exit.*

---

[9]*bow*] literally the bow-shaped piece of wood, which fitted into the yoke beneath the
neck of oxen, but here apparently used for the yoke itself.

[10]*O sweet Oliver*] This was the opening line of a very popular ballad. Only the two lines
("O swete Olyuer Leaue me not behind the[e]") survive elsewhere—in the license for
the publication of the ballad granted by the Stationers' Company to Richard Jones, 6
August, 1584.

[11]*Wind away*] Wend away, depart.

SCENE IV. *The Forest.*

Enter ROSALIND *and* CELIA

ROS. Never talk to me; I will weep.

CEL. Do, I prithee; but yet have the grace to consider that tears do not become a man.

ROS. But have I not cause to weep?

CEL. As good cause as one would desire; therefore weep.

ROS. His very hair is of the dissembling colour.

CEL. Something browner than Judas's:[1] marry, his kisses are Judas's own children.

ROS. I' faith, his hair is of a good colour.

CEL. An excellent colour: your chestnut was ever the only colour.

ROS. And his kissing is as full of sanctity as the touch of holy bread.

CEL. He hath bought a pair of cast[2] lips of Diana: a nun of winter's sisterhood kisses not more religiously; the very ice of chastity is in them.

ROS. But why did he swear he would come this morning, and comes not?

CEL. Nay, certainly, there is no truth in him.

ROS. Do you think so?

CEL. Yes; I think he is not a pick-purse nor a horse-stealer; but for his verity in love, I do think him as concave as a covered goblet[3] or a worm-eaten nut.

ROS. Not true in love?

CEL. Yes, when he is in; but I think he is not in.

ROS. You have heard him swear downright he was.

CEL. "Was" is not "is": besides, the oath of a lover is no stronger than the word of a tapster; they are both the confirmer of false reckonings. He attends here in the forest on the Duke your father.

ROS. I met the Duke yesterday and had much question with him: he asked me of what parentage I was; I told him, of as good as he; so he laughed and let me go. But what talk we of fathers, when there is such a man as Orlando?

CEL. O, that's a brave man! he writes brave verses, speaks brave

---

[1]*browner than Judas's*] Judas was invariably credited with red hair and beard.

[2]*cast*] This is the reading of the First Folio, but the other Folios read *chast*, *i.e.*, chaste. "Cast" was frequently applied to apparel in the sense of "cast off," "left off." This epithet is more in keeping with Celia's banter than the conventional "chaste," which the mention of Diana naturally suggests.

[3]*concave . . . goblet*] a goblet when empty was kept covered.

words, swears brave oaths and breaks them bravely, quite traverse,
athwart the heart of his lover; as a puisny[4] tilter, that spurs his
horse but on one side, breaks his staff[5] like a noble goose: but all's
brave that youth mounts and folly guides. Who comes here?

Enter CORIN

COR.   Mistress and master, you have oft inquired
          After the shepherd that complain'd of love,
          Who you saw sitting by me on the turf,
          Praising the proud disdainful shepherdess
          That was his mistress.
CEL.   Well, and what of him?
COR.   If you will see a pageant truly play'd,
          Between the pale complexion of true love
          And the red glow of scorn and proud disdain,
          Go hence a little and I shall conduct you,
          If you will mark it.
ROS.   O come, let us remove:
          The sight of lovers feedeth those in love.
          Bring us to this sight, and you shall say
          I'll prove a busy actor in their play.   [*Exeunt.*

SCENE V. *Another Part of the Forest.*

Enter SILVIUS *and* PHEBE

SIL.   Sweet Phebe, do not scorn me; do not, Phebe;
          Say that you love me not, but say not so
          In bitterness. The common executioner,
          Whose heart the accustom'd sight of death makes hard,
          Falls not the axe upon the humbled neck

---

[4]*puisny*] This is the old reading. Capell and later editors substitute the more modern
form *puny*. It is used here not in the modern sense of "diminutive," but in that of "having the skill of a novice," "unskilled." The word comes through the French from the
Latin "postnatus," "younger-born."
[5]*breaks his staff*] To break a staff in a tournament across ("quite traverse, athwart," l. 38)
the body of an adversary, and not at push of point, was an accepted sign of clumsy in-
competence. Cf. *All's Well*, II, i, 66, "Good faith, *across*," and *Much Ado*, V, i,
136–137: "this last [staff] was broke *cross*."

But first begs pardon: will you sterner be
Than he that dies and lives[1] by bloody drops?

Enter ROSALIND, CELIA, *and* CORIN, *behind*

PHE.   I would not be thy executioner:
I fly thee, for I would not injure thee.
Thou tell'st me there is murder in mine eye:
'T is pretty, sure, and very probable,
That eyes, that are the frail'st and softest things,
Who shut their coward gates on atomies,[2]
Should be call'd tyrants, butchers, murderers!
Now I do frown on thee with all my heart;
And if mine eyes can wound, now let them kill thee:
Now counterfeit to swoon; why now fall down;
Or if thou canst not, O, for shame, for shame,
Lie not, to say mine eyes are murderers!
Now show the wound mine eye hath made in thee:
Scratch thee but with a pin, and there remains
Some scar of it; lean but upon a rush,
The cicatrice and capable impressure[3]
Thy palm some moment keeps; but now mine eyes,
Which I have darted at thee, hurt thee not,
Nor, I am sure, there is no force in eyes
That can do hurt.
SIL.   O dear Phebe,
If ever,—as that ever may be near,—
You meet in some fresh cheek the power of fancy,
Then shall you know the wounds invisible
That love's keen arrows make.
PHE.   But till that time
Come not thou near me: and when that time comes,
Afflict me with thy mocks, pity me not;
As till that time I shall not pity thee.
ROS.   And why, I pray you? Who might be your mother,
That you insult, exult, and all at once,
Over the wretched? What though you have no beauty,—
As, by my faith, I see no more in you
Than without candle may go dark to bed,—

---

[1] *dies and lives*] This is a common inversion of the more ordinary phrase "lives and dies,"
i.e., subsists from the cradle to the grave. Cf. Barclay's *Ship of Fooles*, 1570, f. 67: "He
is a foole, and so shall he *dye and live*."
[2] *atomies*] Cf. III, ii, 217, *supra*.
[3] *The cicatrice . . . impressure*] The scar, or mark, and perceptible or sensible impression.

Must you be therefore proud and pitiless?
Why, what means this? Why do you look on me?
I see no more in you than in the ordinary
Of nature's sale-work.[4] 'Od's my little life,
I think she means to tangle my eyes too!
No, faith, proud mistress, hope not after it:
'T is not your inky brows, your black silk hair,
Your bugle[5] eyeballs, nor your cheek of cream,
That can entame my spirits to your worship.
You foolish shepherd, wherefore do you follow her,
Like foggy south, puffing with wind and rain?[6]
You are a thousand times a properer man
Than she a woman: 't is such fools as you
That makes the world full of ill-favour'd children:
'T is not her glass, but you, that flatters her;
And out of you she sees herself more proper
Than any of her lineaments can show her.
But, mistress, know yourself: down on your knees,
And thank heaven, fasting, for a good man's love:
For I must tell you friendly in your ear,
Sell when you can: you are not for all markets:
Cry the man mercy; love him; take his offer:
Foul is most foul, being foul to be a scoffer.[7]
So take her to thee, shepherd: fare you well.

PHE.   Sweet youth, I pray you, chide a year together:
I had rather hear you chide than this man woo.

ROS.   He's fallen in love with your foulness and she'll fall in love with
my anger. If it be so, as fast as she answers thee with frowning
looks, I'll sauce her with bitter words. Why look you so upon me?

PHE.   For no ill will I bear you.

ROS.   I pray you, do not fall in love with me,
For I am falser than vows made in wine:
Besides, I like you not. If you will know my house,
'T is at the tuft of olives here hard by.
Will you go, sister? Shepherd, ply her hard.
Come, sister. Shepherdess, look on him better,
And be not proud: though all the world could see,

---

[4]*sale-work*] ready-made goods.
[5]*bugle*] black, from the tube-shaped glass bead, commonly of that colour, used to or-
nament wearing apparel.
[6]*foggy south . . . rain*] The foggy southern quarter of the sky, which generates wind and
rain. Cf. *Rom. and Jul.*, I, iv, 103: "the *dewdropping south.*"
[7]*Foul . . . scoffer*] An ugly woman exaggerates her ugliness when she grows scornful.

None could be so abused in sight as he.
Come, to our flock.   [*Exeunt* ROSALIND, CELIA, *and* CORIN.
PHE.   Dead shepherd, now I find thy saw of might,
   "Who ever loved that loved not at first sight?"[8]
SIL.   Sweet Phebe,—
PHE.   Ha, what say'st thou, Silvius?
SIL.   Sweet Phebe, pity me.
PHE.   Why, I am sorry for thee, gentle Silvius.
SIL.   Wherever sorrow is, relief would be:
   If you do sorrow at my grief in love,
   By giving love your sorrow and my grief
   Were both extermined.
PHE.   Thou hast my love: is not that neighbourly?
SIL.   I would have you.
PHE.   Why, that were covetousness.
   Silvius, the time was that I hated thee,
   And yet it is not that I bear thee love;
   But since that thou canst talk of love so well,
   Thy company, which erst was irksome to me,
   I will endure, and I'll employ thee too:
   But do not look for further recompense
   Than thine own gladness that thou art employ'd.
SIL.   So holy and so perfect is my love,
   And I in such a poverty of grace,
   That I shall think it a most plenteous crop
   To glean the broken ears after the man
   That the main harvest reaps: loose now and then
   A scatter'd smile, and that I'll live upon.
PHE.   Know'st thou the youth that spoke to me erewhile?
SIL.   Not very well, but I have met him oft;
   And he hath bought the cottage and the bounds
   That the old carlot[9] once was master of.
PHE.   Think not I love him, though I ask for him;
   'T is but a peevish boy; yet he talks well;
   But what care I for words? yet words do well
   When he that speaks them pleases those that hear.
   It is a pretty youth: not very pretty:

---

[8]*Dead shepherd . . . sight*] The "dead shepherd" is Christopher Marlowe, who died in
   1593. The line, "Who ever loved," etc., is from Marlowe's popular translation of the
   pseudo-Musaeus' Greek poem, *Hero and Leander* (Sest. I, 1. 176), first printed in
   1598.
[9]*carlot*] Apparently a diminutive of "carl," churl, peasant. No other example of the word
   is found.

But, sure, he's proud, and yet his pride becomes him:
He'll make a proper man: the best thing in him
Is his complexion; and faster than his tongue
Did make offence his eye did heal it up.
He is not very tall; yet for his years he's tall:
His leg is but so so; and yet 't is well:
There was a pretty redness in his lip,
A little riper and more lusty red
Than that mix'd in his cheek; 't was just the difference
Betwixt the constant red and mingled damask.[10]
There be some women, Silvius, had they mark'd him
In parcels as I did, would have gone near
To fall in love with him: but, for my part,
I love him not nor hate him not; and yet
I have more cause to hate him than to love him:
For what had he to do to chide at me?
He said mine eyes were black and my hair black;
And, now I am remember'd, scorn'd at me:
I marvel why I answer'd not again:
But that's all one; omittance is no quittance.[11]
I'll write to him a very taunting letter,
And thou shalt bear it: wilt thou, Silvius?

SIL.   Phebe, with all my heart.

PHE.   I'll write it straight;
The matter 's in my head and in my heart:
I will be bitter with him and passing short.
Go with me, Sylvius.   [*Exeunt.*

---

[10]*mingled damask*] Cf. *Sonnet* cxxx, 5: "I have seen roses *damask'd*, red and white."
[11]*omittance is no quittance*] Milton, *Paradise Lost*, X, 53, varies this expression thus:
    "Forbearance is no quittance." Quittance means discharge.

ACT IV.

Scene I. *The Forest.*

Enter Rosalind, Celia, *and* Jaques

Jaques.   I prithee, pretty youth, let me be better acquainted with thee.

Ros.   They say you are a melancholy fellow.

Jaq.   I am so; I do love it better than laughing.

Ros.   Those that are in extremity of either are abominable fellows, and betray themselves to every modern censure[1] worse than drunkards.

Jaq.   Why, 't is good to be sad and say nothing.

Ros.   Why then, 't is good to be a post.

Jaq.   I have neither the scholar's melancholy, which is emulation; nor the musician's, which is fantastical; nor the courtier's, which is proud; nor the soldier's, which is ambitious; nor the lawyer's, which is politic; nor the lady's, which is nice; nor the lover's, which is all these: but it is a melancholy of mine own, compounded of many simples, extracted from many objects; and indeed the sundry contemplation of my travels, in which my often rumination wraps me in a most humorous sadness.

Ros.   A traveller! By my faith, you have great reason to be sad: I fear you have sold your own lands to see other men's; then, to have seen much, and to have nothing, is to have rich eyes[2] and poor hands.

Jaq.   Yes, I have gained my experience.

Ros.   And your experience makes you sad: I had rather have a fool to make me merry than experience to make me sad; and to travel for it too!

Enter Orlando

[1] *modern censure*] common, ordinary judgment.
[2] *rich eyes*] Cf. *All's Well,* V, iii, 16–17: "the survey Of *richest eyes.*"

55

ORL. Good day and happiness, dear Rosalind!

JAQ. Nay, then, God buy you,³ an you talk in blank verse. [*Exit.*

ROS. Farewell, Monsieur Traveller: look you lisp and wear strange suits; disable all the benefits of your own country; be out of love with your nativity and almost chide God for making you that countenance you are; or I will scarce think you have swam in a gondola.⁴ Why, how now, Orlando! where have you been all this while? You a lover! An you serve me such another trick, never come in my sight more.

ORL. My fair Rosalind, I come within an hour of my promise.

ROS. Break an hour's promise in love! He that will divide a minute into a thousand parts, and break but a part of the thousandth part of a minute in the affairs of love, it may be said of him that Cupid hath clapped him o' the shoulder, but I'll warrant him heart-whole.

ORL. Pardon me, dear Rosalind.

ROS. Nay, an you be so tardy, come no more in my sight: I had as lief be wooed of a snail.

ORL. Of a snail?

ROS. Ay, of a snail; for though he comes slowly, he carries his house on his head; a better jointure, I think, than you make a woman: besides, he brings his destiny with him.

ORL. What's that?

ROS. Why, horns, which such as you are fain to be beholding to your wives for: but he comes armed in his fortune and prevents the slander of his wife.

ORL. Virtue is no horn-maker; and my Rosalind is virtuous.

ROS. And I am your Rosalind.

CEL. It pleases him to call you so; but he hath a Rosalind of a better leer than you.

ROS. Come, woo me, woo me; for now I am in a holiday humour and like enough to consent. What would you say to me now, an I were your very very Rosalind?

ORL. I would kiss before I spoke.

ROS. Nay, you were better speak first; and when you were gravelled for lack of matter, you might take occasion to kiss. Very good orators, when they are out, they will spit; and for lovers lacking—God warn us!—matter, the cleanliest shift is to kiss.

ORL. How if the kiss be denied?

ROS. Then she puts you to entreaty and there begins new matter.

³*God buy you*] Cf. III, ii, 242, *supra.*
⁴*swam in a gondola*] been on a visit to Venice, the fashionable goal of contemporary travel.

ORL.   Who could be out, being before his beloved mistress?

ROS.   Marry, that should you, if I were your mistress, or I should think my honesty ranker than my wit.

ORL.   What, of my suit?

ROS.   Not out of your apparel, and yet out of your suit. Am not I your Rosalind?

ORL.   I take some joy to say you are, because I would be talking of her.

ROS.   Well, in her person, I say I will not have you.

ORL.   Then in mine own person I die.

ROS.   No, faith, die by attorney.[5] The poor world is almost six thousand years old, and in all this time there was not any man died in his own person, videlicet, in a love-cause. Troilus had his brains dashed out with a Grecian club; yet he did what he could to die before, and he is one of the patterns of love. Leander, he would have lived many a fair year, though Hero had turned nun, if it had not been for a hot midsummer night; for, good youth, he went but forth to wash him in the Hellespont and being taken with the cramp was drowned: and the foolish chroniclers[6] of that age found it was "Hero of Sestos." But these are all lies: men have died from time to time and worms have eaten them, but not for love.

ORL.   I would not have my right Rosalind of this mind; for, I protest, her frown might kill me.

ROS.   By this hand, it will not kill a fly. But come, now I will be your Rosalind in a more coming-on disposition, and ask me what you will, I will grant it.

ORL.   Then love me, Rosalind.

ROS.   Yes, faith, will I, Fridays and Saturdays and all.

ORL.   And wilt thou have me?

ROS.   Ay, and twenty such.

ORL.   What sayest thou?

ROS.   Are you not good?

ORL.   I hope so.

ROS.   Why then, can one desire too much of a good thing? Come, sister, you shall be the priest and marry us. Give me your hand, Orlando. What do you say, sister?

ORL.   Pray thee, marry us.

CEL.   I cannot say the words.

ROS.   You must begin, "Will you, Orlando—"

---

[5]*by attorney*] by deputy. Cf. *Rich. III*, V, iii, 83: "I, *by attorney*, bless thee from thy mother."

[6]*chroniclers*] This is the reading of the Folios. It was needlessly changed by Hanmer to *coroners*, which the use of the word "found," *i.e.* "gave the finding or verdict," only speciously supports.

CEL.   Go to. Will you, Orlando, have to wife this Rosalind?

ORL.   I will.

ROS.   Ay, but when?

ORL.   Why now; as fast as she can marry us.

ROS.   Then you must say "I take thee, Rosalind, for wife."

ORL.   I take thee, Rosalind, for wife.

ROS.   I might ask you for your commission; but I do take thee, Orlando, for my husband: there's a girl goes before the priest;[7] and certainly a woman's thought runs before her actions.

ORL.   So do all thoughts; they are winged.

ROS.   Now tell me how long you would have her after you have possessed her.

ORL.   For ever and a day.

ROS.   Say "a day," without the "ever." No, no, Orlando, men are April when they woo, December when they wed: maids are May when they are maids, but the sky changes when they are wives. I will be more jealous of thee than a Barbary cock-pigeon[8] over his hen, more clamorous than a parrot against rain, more new-fangled[9] than an ape, more giddy in my desires than a monkey: I will weep for nothing, like Diana in the fountain,[10] and I will do that when you are disposed to be merry; I will laugh like a hyen, and that when thou art inclined to sleep.

ORL.   But will my Rosalind do so?

ROS.   By my life, she will do as I do.

ORL.   O, but she is wise.

ROS.   Or else she could not have the wit to do this: the wiser, the waywarder: make the doors upon a woman's wit and it will out at the casement; shut that and 't will out at the key-hole; stop that, 't will fly with the smoke out at the chimney.

ORL.   A man that had a wife with such a wit, he might say "Wit, whither wilt?"[11]

ROS.   Nay, you might keep that check for it till you met your wife's wit going to your neighbour's bed.

ORL.   And what wit could wit have to excuse that?

---

[7]*there 's a girl . . . priest*] Rosalind admits that the bride is anticipating the part in the ceremony that belongs to Celia, who acts as priest.

[8]*Barbary cock-pigeon*] This bird, now known as a "barb," is of black colour, and was introduced from North Africa. Cf. *2 Hen. IV*, II, iv, 94: "*Barbary* hen."

[9]*new-fangled*] fond of what is new. Cf. Cotgrave's *Fr.-Eng. Dict.*: "Fantastique, humorous, *new-fangled*, giddie, skittish."

[10]*like . . . fountain*] A possible allusion to an "alabaster image of Diana," which, according to Stow, was set up near the cross at West Cheap, London, with "water conveyed from the Thames prilling from her naked breast."

[11]*Wit, whither wilt?*] Cf. I, ii, 51, *supra.*

Ros.   Marry, to say she came to seek you there. You shall never take
       her without her answer, unless you take her without her tongue.
       O, that woman that cannot make her fault her husband's occa-
       sion,[12] let her never nurse her child herself, for she will breed it
       like a fool!
ORL.   For these two hours, Rosalind, I will leave thee.
Ros.   Alas, dear love, I cannot lack thee two hours!
ORL.   I must attend the Duke at dinner: by two o'clock I will be with
       thee again.
Ros.   Ay, go your ways, go your ways; I knew what you would prove:
       my friends told me as much, and I thought no less: that flattering
       tongue of yours won me: 't is but one cast away, and so, come,
       death! Two o'clock is your hour?
ORL.   Ay, sweet Rosalind.
Ros.   By my troth, and in good earnest, and so God mend me, and by
       all pretty oaths that are not dangerous, if you break one jot of your
       promise or come one minute behind your hour, I will think you
       the most pathetical[13] break-promise, and the most hollow lover,
       and the most unworthy of her you call Rosalind, that may be cho-
       sen out of the gross band of the unfaithful: therefore beware my
       censure and keep your promise.
ORL.   With no less religion than if thou wert indeed my Rosalind: so
       adieu.
Ros.   Well, Time is the old justice that examines all such offenders,
       and let Time try: adieu.   [*Exit* ORLANDO.
CEL.   You have simply misused our sex in your love-prate: we must
       have your doublet and hose plucked over your head, and show the
       world what the bird hath done to her own nest.
Ros.   O coz, coz, coz, my pretty little coz, that thou didst know how
       many fathom deep I am in love! But it cannot be sounded: my af-
       fection hath an unknown bottom, like the bay of Portugal.[14]
CEL.   Or rather, bottomless; that as fast as you pour affection in, it
       runs out.
Ros.   No, that same wicked bastard of Venus that was begot of
       thought, conceived of spleen, and born of madness, that blind

---

[12]*make . . . occasion*] represent her fault to be occasioned by her husband, or make her
   fault the opportunity of taking advantage of her husband. The reading, though often
   questioned, is probably right.
[13]*pathetical*] The word, though often meaning "impassioned," or "persuasive," seems to
   acquire here a touch of scorn, and is almost equivalent to "pitiful." Cf. *L. L. L.*, IV, i,
   141: "A most *pathetical* wit."
[14]*bay of Portugal*] Sailors bestowed this title on the sea off the Portuguese coast between
   Oporto and Cintra. The water there attained a depth of 1400 fathoms within 42 miles
   of the shore.

rascally boy that abuses every one's eyes because his own are out,
let him be judge how deep I am in love. I'll tell thee, Aliena, I cannot be out of the sight of Orlando: I'll go find a shadow[15] and sigh
till he come.

CEL.   And I'll sleep.   [*Exeunt.*

SCENE II. *The Forest.*

Enter JAQUES, Lords, *and* Foresters

JAQ.   Which is he that killed the deer?

A LORD.   Sir, it was I.

JAQ.   Let 's present him to the Duke, like a Roman conqueror; and it
would do well to set the deer's horns upon his head, for a branch
of victory. Have you no song, forester, for this purpose?

FOR.   Yes, sir.

JAQ.   Sing it: 't is no matter how it be in tune, so it make noise enough.

SONG

FOR.   What shall he have that kill'd the deer?
                           His leather skin and horns to wear.
                                   Then sing him home:[1]
                                       [*The rest shall bear this burden.*
                           Take thou no scorn to wear the horn;
                           It was a crest ere thou wast born:
                                   Thy father's father wore it,
                                   And thy father bore it:
                           The horn, the horn, the lusty horn
                           Is not a thing to laugh to scorn.   [*Exeunt.*

---

[15]*shadow*] shade, or shady place. Cf. *Tempest,* IV, i, 66–67: "Broom-groves, Whose
shadow the dismissed bachelor loves."

[1]*Then sing him home:*] In the Folios these words, together with those here printed as the
appended stage direction, form a single line of the song. Theobald first made the
change which is adopted here. A few editors read, *They sing him home,* and include
these words along with those which follow in the stage direction. The song appears
with music in John Hilton's *Catch that catch can,* 1652. The particular words with
which this note deals are all omitted. Hilton is doubtfully identified with a famous musician of the same name, who was Shakespeare's contemporary.

SCENE III. *The Forest.*

Enter ROSALIND *and* CELIA

ROS.   How say you now? Is it not past two o'clock? and here much
    Orlando![1]
CEL.   I warrant you, with pure love and troubled brain, he hath ta'en his
    bow and arrows and is gone forth to sleep. Look, who comes here.

Enter SILVIUS

SIL.   My errand is to you, fair youth;
    My gentle Phebe bid me give you this:
    I know not the contents: but, as I guess
    By the stern brow and waspish action
    Which she did use as she was writing of it,
    It bears an angry tenour: pardon me;
    I am but as a guiltless messenger.
ROS.   Patience herself would startle at this letter
    And play the swaggerer; bear this, bear all:
    She says I am not fair, that I lack manners;
    She calls me proud, and that she could not love me,
    Were man as rare as phœnix.[2] 'Od's my will!
    Her love is not the hare that I do hunt:
    Why writes she so to me? Well, shepherd, well,
    This is a letter of your own device.
SIL.   No, I protest, I know not the contents:
    Phebe did write it.
ROS.   Come, come, you are a fool,
    And turn'd into the extremity of love.
    I saw her hand: she has a leathern hand,
    A freestone-colour'd[3] hand; I verily did think
    That her old gloves were on, but 't was her hands:
    She has a huswife's hand; but that's no matter:
    I say she never did invent this letter;
    This is a man's invention and his hand.

---

[1]*and here much Orlando*] An ironical use of "much," implying just the opposite of what
  the word means: "we find much of, a great deal of, Orlando here," *i.e.*, "he is not here
  at all." Cf. the colloquialism, "I shall get much [*verè*—nothing] by that."
[2]*as rare as phœnix*] The phœnix is commonly described in classical poetry as unique.
  Cf. Ovid's *Amores*, II, vi, 54, "vivax phœnix, *unica* semper avis." Cf. *Tempest*, III, iii,
  23: "There is one tree, the phœnix' throne; *one phœnix.*"
[3]*freestone-colour'd*] brownish yellow, like bath brick.

SIL.　Sure, it is hers.

ROS.　Why, 't is a boisterous and a cruel style,
　　　A style for challengers; why, she defies me,
　　　Like Turk to Christian: women's gentle brain
　　　Could not drop forth such giant-rude invention,
　　　Such Ethiope[4] words, blacker in their effect
　　　Than in their countenance. Will you hear the letter?

SIL.　So please you, for I never heard it yet;
　　　Yet heard too much of Phebe's cruelty.

ROS.　She Phebes me: mark how the tyrant writes.

[*Reads*]　　　　　　Art thou god to shepherd turn'd,
　　　　　　　　　That a maiden's heart hath burn'd?

Can a woman rail thus?

SIL.　Call you this railing?

ROS.　[*reads*]

　　　　　　　Why, thy godhead laid apart,
　　　　　　　Warr'st thou with a woman's heart?

Did you ever hear such railing?

　　　　　　　Whiles the eye of man did woo me,
　　　　　　　That could do no vengeance to me.

Meaning me a beast.

　　　　　　　If the scorn of your bright eyne
　　　　　　　Have power to raise such love in mine,
　　　　　　　Alack, in me what strange effect
　　　　　　　Would they work in mild aspect![5]
　　　　　　　Whiles you chid me, I did love;
　　　　　　　How then might your prayers move!
　　　　　　　He that brings this love to thee
　　　　　　　Little knows this love in me:
　　　　　　　And by him seal up thy mind;[6]
　　　　　　　Whether that thy youth and kind[7]
　　　　　　　Will the faithful offer take
　　　　　　　Of me and all that I can make;
　　　　　　　Or else by him my love deny,
　　　　　　　And then I'll study how to die.

[4]*Ethiope*] this is the only example of the adjectival use of this word, which is frequently
　found elsewhere as a noun, meaning "a swarthy person."

[5]*aspect*] This word, which is always accented on the last syllable in Shakespeare, is here
　an astrological term denoting the appearance of the planets. Cf. *Wint. Tale*, II, i,
　106–107: "the heavens look With an *aspéct* more favourable."

[6]*seal up thy mind*] seal up your decision, and send it back by him.

[7]*youth and kind*] youth and nature, the natural sentiment of youth.

SIL.   Call you this chiding?
CEL.   Alas, poor shepherd!
ROS.   Do you pity him? no, he deserves no pity. Wilt thou love such
       a woman? What, to make thee an instrument and play false strains
       upon thee! not to be endured! Well, go your way to her, for I see
       love hath made thee a tame snake, and say this to her: that if she
       love me, I charge her to love thee; if she will not, I will never have
       her unless thou entreat for her. If you be a true lover, hence, and
       not a word; for here comes more company.   [*Exit* SILVIUS.

Enter OLIVER

OLI.   Good morrow, fair ones: pray you, if you know,
       Where in the purlieus of this forest stands
       A sheep-cote fenced about with olive-trees?
CEL.   West of this place, down in the neighbour bottom:
       The rank of osiers by the murmuring stream
       Left on your right hand brings you to the place.
       But at this hour the house doth keep itself;
       There 's none within.
OLI.   If that an eye may profit by a tongue,
       Then should I know you by description;
       Such garments and such years: "The boy is fair,
       Of female favour, and bestows himself[8]
       Like a ripe sister:[9] the woman low,
       And browner than her brother." Are not you
       The owner of the house I did inquire for?
CEL.   It is no boast, being ask'd, to say we are.
OLI.   Orlando doth commend him to you both,
       And to that youth he calls his Rosalind
       He sends this bloody napkin.[10] Are you he?
ROS.   I am: what must we understand by this?
OLI.   Some of my shame; if you will know of me
       What man I am, and how, and why, and where
       This handkercher was stain'd.
CEL.   I pray you, tell it.
OLI.   When last the young Orlando parted from you

[8]*bestows himself*] deports himself, behaves, as in 2 *Hen. IV*, II, ii, 163–164: "How might
we see Falstaff *bestow himself* to-night in his true colours."
[9]*Like a ripe sister*] This, the original reading, leaves the line metrically imperfect. A syllable seems lacking after "sister." But such an irregularity is not uncommon. With a
view to correcting the metre, and removing the ambiguity of "ripe sister," *right forester*
has been substituted. "Like a ripe sister" may be correct, and may mean that Rosalind
treats Celia like a mature, elder kinswoman.
[10]*napkin*] This is the "handkercher" or "handkerchief" of line 96, *infra*.

He left a promise to return again
Within an hour, and pacing through the forest,
Chewing the food of sweet and bitter fancy,
Lo, what befel! he threw his eye aside,
And mark what object did present itself:
Under an oak,[11] whose boughs were moss'd with age
And high top bald with dry antiquity,
A wretched ragged man, o'ergrown with hair,
Lay sleeping on his back: about his neck
A green and gilded snake had wreathed itself,
Who with her head nimble in threats approach'd
The opening of his mouth; but suddenly,
Seeing Orlando, it unlink'd itself,
And with indented glides[12] did slip away
Into a bush: under which bush's shade
A lioness, with udders all drawn dry,
Lay couching, head on ground, with catlike watch,
When that the sleeping man should stir; for 't is
The royal disposition of that beast
To prey on nothing that doth seem as dead:
This seen, Orlando did approach the man
And found it was his brother, his elder brother.

CEL.   O, I have heard him speak of that same brother;
And he did render him the most unnatural
That lived amongst men.

OLI.   And well he might so do,
For well I know he was unnatural.

ROS.   But, to Orlando: did he leave him there,
Food to the suck'd and hungry lioness?

OLI.   Twice did he turn his back and purposed so;
But kindness, nobler ever than revenge,
And nature, stronger than his just occasion,[13]
Made him give battle to the lioness,
Who quickly fell before him: in which hurtling
From miserable slumber I awaked.

CEL.   Are you his brother?

ROS.   Was 't you he rescued?

---

[11]*oak*] The Folios insert *old* before *oak*, but metrical considerations almost compel its
omission, which Pope first proposed.

[12]*indented glides*] sinuous glidings. Cf. "*indented* wave" of the movement of the serpent
in Milton's *Paradise Lost*, IX, 496.

[13]*just occasion*] the just ground which would have warranted Orlando in abandoning
his brother.

CEL.   Was 't you that did so oft contrive to kill him?
OLI.   'T was I; but 't is not I: I do not shame
       To tell you what I was, since my conversion
       So sweetly tastes, being the thing I am.
ROS.   But, for the bloody napkin?
OLI.   By and by.
       When from the first to last betwixt us two
       Tears our recountments had most kindly bathed,
       As[14] how I came into that desert place;
       In brief, he led me to the gentle Duke,
       Who gave me fresh array and entertainment,
       Committing me unto my brother's love;
       Who led me instantly unto his cave,
       There stripp'd himself, and here upon his arm
       The lioness had torn some flesh away,
       Which all this while had bled; and now he fainted
       And cried, in fainting, upon Rosalind.
       Brief, I recover'd him, bound up his wound;
       And, after some small space, being strong at heart,
       He sent me hither, stranger as I am,
       To tell this story, that you might excuse
       His broken promise, and to give this napkin,
       Dyed in his blood, unto the shepherd youth
       That he in sport doth call his Rosalind.
                                        [ROSALIND *swoons.*
CEL.   Why, how now, Ganymede! sweet Ganymede!
OLI.   Many will swoon when they do look on blood.
CEL.   There is more in it. Cousin Ganymede!
OLI.   Look, he recovers.
ROS.   I would I were at home.
CEL.   We'll lead you thither.
       I pray you, will you take him by the arm?
OLI.   Be of good cheer, youth: you a man! you lack a man's heart.
ROS.   I do so, I confess it. Ah, sirrah, a body would think this was well
       counterfeited! I pray you, tell your brother how well I counter-
       feited. Heigh-ho!
OLI.   This was not counterfeit: there is too great testimony in your
       complexion that it was a passion of earnest.
ROS.   Counterfeit, I assure you.
OLI.   Well then, take a good heart and counterfeit to be a man.
ROS.   So I do: but, i' faith, I should have been a woman by right.

---

[14]*As*] As for instance.

CEL. Come, you look paler and paler: pray you, draw homewards.
  Good sir, go with us.
OLI. That will I, for I must bear answer back
  How you excuse my brother, Rosalind.
ROS. I shall devise something: but, I pray you, commend my coun-
  terfeiting to him. Will you go?   [*Exeunt.*

ACT V.

Scene I. *The Forest.*

Enter Touchstone *and* Audrey

Touchstone. We shall find a time, Audrey; patience, gentle Audrey.

Aud. Faith, the priest was good enough, for all the old gentleman's saying.

Touch. A most wicked Sir Oliver, Audrey, a most vile Martext. But, Audrey, there is a youth here in the forest lays claim to you.

Aud. Ay, I know who 't is: he hath no interest in me in the world: here comes the man you mean.

Touch. It is meat and drink[1] to me to see a clown: by my troth, we that have good wits have much to answer for; we shall be flouting; we cannot hold.[2]

Enter William

Will. Good even, Audrey.

Aud. God ye good even, William.

Will. And good even to you, sir.

Touch. Good even, gentle friend. Cover thy head, cover thy head; nay, prithee, be covered. How old are you, friend?

Will. Five and twenty, sir.

Touch. A ripe age. Is thy name William?

Will. William, sir.

Touch. A fair name. Wast born i' the forest here?

Will. Ay, sir, I thank God.

Touch. "Thank God;" a good answer. Art rich?

Will. Faith, sir, so so.

---

[1]*meat and drink*] a proverbial expression implying something very congenial. Cf. *M. Wives*, I, i, 268: "That's *meat and drink* to me."

[2]*hold*] restrain (*sc.* our wit).

67

TOUCH. "So so" is good, very good, very excellent good; and yet it is not; it is but so so. Art thou wise?

WILL. Ay, sir, I have a pretty wit.

TOUCH. Why, thou sayest well. I do now remember a saying, "The fool doth think he is wise, but the wise man knows himself to be a fool." The heathen philosopher, when he had a desire to eat a grape, would open his lips when he put it into his mouth; meaning thereby that grapes were made to eat and lips to open. You do love this maid?

WILL. I do, sir.

TOUCH. Give me your hand. Art thou learned?

WILL. No, sir.

TOUCH. Then learn this of me: to have, is to have; for it is a figure in rhetoric that drink, being poured out of a cup into a glass, by filling the one doth empty the other; for all your writers do consent that ipse is he: now, you are not ipse, for I am he.

WILL. Which he, sir?

TOUCH. He, sir, that must marry this woman. Therefore, you clown, abandon,—which is in the vulgar leave,—the society,—which in the boorish is company,—of this female,—which in the common is woman; which together is, abandon the society of this female, or, clown, thou perishest; or, to thy better understanding, diest; or, to wit, I kill thee, make thee away, translate thy life into death, thy liberty into bondage: I will deal in poison with thee, or in bastinado,[3] or in steel; I will bandy[4] with thee in faction; I will o'er-run thee with policy; I will kill thee a hundred and fifty ways: therefore tremble, and depart.

AUD. Do, good William.

WILL. God rest you merry, sir. [*Exit.*

Enter CORIN

COR. Our master and mistress seeks you; come, away, away!

TOUCH. Trip, Audrey! trip, Audrey! I attend, I attend. [*Exeunt.*

---

[3]*bastinado*] cudgelling. Cf. Florio's *Ital.-Eng. Dict.*: "A *bastonado*, or cudgell-blow."
[4]*bandy*] The word literally means "to toss from side to side like a tennis-ball"; but it is here synonymous with "contend" or "fight."

SCENE II. *The Forest.*

Enter ORLANDO *and* OLIVER

ORL.   Is 't possible that on so little acquaintance you should like her? that but seeing you should love her? and loving woo? and, wooing, she should grant? and will you persever to enjoy her?

OLI.   Neither call the giddiness of it in question, the poverty of her, the small acquaintance, my sudden wooing, nor her sudden consenting; but say with me, I love Aliena; say with her that she loves me; consent with both that we may enjoy each other: it shall be to your good; for my father's house and all the revenue that was old Sir Rowland's will I estate upon you, and here live and die a shepherd.

ORL.   You have my consent. Let your wedding be to-morrow: thither will I invite the Duke and all's contented followers. Go you and prepare Aliena; for look you, here comes my Rosalind.

Enter ROSALIND

ROS.   God save you, brother.

OLI.   And you, fair sister.[1]   [*Exit.*

ROS.   O, my dear Orlando, how it grieves me to see thee wear thy heart in a scarf![2]

ORL.   It is my arm.

ROS.   I thought thy heart had been wounded with the claws of a lion.

ORL.   Wounded it is, but with the eyes of a lady.

ROS.   Did your brother tell you how I counterfeited to swoon when he showed me your handkercher?

ORL.   Ay, and greater wonders than that.

ROS.   O, I know where you are: nay, 't is true: there was never any thing so sudden but the fight of two rams, and Caesar's thrasonical brag of "I came, saw, and overcame:" for your brother and my sister no sooner met but they looked; no sooner looked but they loved; no sooner loved but they sighed; no sooner sighed but they asked one another the reason; no sooner knew the reason but they sought the remedy: and in these degrees have they made a pair of stairs to marriage which they will climb incontinent, or

---

[1]*fair sister*] Rosalind is still disguised, and, as far as is known, Oliver believes her to be a boy. But he enters into Orlando's humour, and calls her "sister" in the spirit of Act IV, Sc. i. Cf. IV, iii, 86, where Oliver has already likened the boy Rosalind to "a *ripe sister.*"

[2]*in a scarf*] in a sling.

else be incontinent before marriage: they are in the very wrath of love and they will together; clubs cannot part them.

ORL. They shall be married to-morrow, and I will bid the Duke to the nuptial.[3] But, O, how bitter a thing it is to look into happiness through another man's eyes! By so much the more shall I to-morrow be at the height of heart-heaviness, by how much I shall think my brother happy in having what he wishes for.

ROS. Why then, to-morrow I cannot serve your turn for Rosalind?

ORL. I can live no longer by thinking.

ROS. I will weary you then no longer with idle talking. Know of me then, for now I speak to some purpose, that I know you are a gentleman of good conceit: I speak not this that you should bear a good opinion of my knowledge, insomuch I say I know you are; neither do I labour for a greater esteem than may in some little measure draw a belief from you, to do yourself good and not to grace me. Believe then, if you please, that I can do strange things: I have, since I was three year old, conversed with a magician, most profound in his art and yet not damnable. If you do love Rosalind so near the heart as your gesture cries it out, when your brother marries Aliena, shall you marry her: I know into what straits of fortune she is driven; and it is not impossible to me, if it appear not inconvenient to you, to set her before your eyes to-morrow human as she is and without any danger.

ORL. Speakest thou in sober meanings?

ROS. By my life, I do; which I tender dearly, though I say I am a magician.[4] Therefore, put you in your best array; bid your friends; for if you will be married to-morrow, you shall; and to Rosalind, if you will.

Enter SILVIUS *and* PHEBE

Look, here comes a lover of mine and a lover of hers.

PHE. Youth, you have done me much ungentleness,
To show the letter that I writ to you.

ROS. I care not if I have: it is my study
To seem despiteful and ungentle to you:
You are there followed by a faithful shepherd;
Look upon him, love him; he worships you.

PHE. Good shepherd, tell this youth what 't is to love.

SIL. It is to be all made of sighs and tears;

---

[3]*nuptial*] Shakespeare invariably uses the singular. The plural, "nuptials," is a more modern usage. Conversely he employs "funerals" where we use "funeral."

[4]*By my life . . . . magician*] By statute law, 5 Eliz., Cap. 16, practisers of witchcraft were liable to punishment by death.

And so am I for Phebe.
PHE.   And I for Ganymede.
ORL.   And I for Rosalind.
ROS.   And I for no woman.
SIL.   It is to be all made of faith and service;
       And so am I for Phebe.
PHE.   And I for Ganymede.
ORL.   And I for Rosalind.
ROS.   And I for no woman.
SIL.   It is to be all made of fantasy,
       All made of passion, and all made of wishes;
       All adoration, duty, and observance,[5]
       All humbleness, all patience, and impatience,
       All purity, all trial, all observance;
       And so am I for Phebe.
PHE.   And so am I for Ganymede.
ORL.   And so am I for Rosalind.
ROS.   And so am I for no woman.
PHE.   If this be so, why blame you me to love you?
SIL.   If this be so, why blame you me to love you?
ORL.   If this be so, why blame you me to love you?
ROS.   Why do you speak too, "Why blame you me to love you?"
ORL.   To her that is not here, nor doth not hear.
ROS.   Pray you, no more of this; 't is like the howling of Irish wolves
       against the moon.[6] [*To Sil.*] I will help you, if I can: [*To Phe.*] I
       would love you, if I could. To-morrow meet me all together. [*To
       Phe.*] I will marry you, if ever I marry woman, and I'll be married
       to-morrow: [*To Orl.*] I will satisfy you, if ever I satisfied man, and
       you shall be married to-morrow: [*To Sil.*] I will content you, if
       what pleases you contents you, and you shall be married to-
       morrow. [*To Orl.*] As you love Rosalind, meet: [*To Sil.*] as you love
       Phebe, meet: and as I love no woman, I'll meet. So, fare you well:
       I have left you commands.
SIL.   I'll not fail, if I live.
PHE.   Nor I.
ORL.   Nor I.   [*Exeunt.*

[5]*observance*] The repetition of this word at the end of the next line but one below suggests that one or other of the two "observances" is wrongly printed. The word seems
somewhat more closely connected with "adoration" and "duty" as here, than with "pu-
rity" and "trial" as in line 91. Malone suggested *obedience* in the second place. Others
prefer Ritson's conjecture of *obeisance*.
[6]*howling . . . moon*] Cf. Lodge's *Romance of Rosalynd:* "Thou barkest with the *wolves* of
Syria *against the moone.*" Wolves abounded in Ireland, and the substitution of the epithet *Irish* for *of Syria* is quite natural.

SCENE III. *The Forest.*

Enter TOUCHSTONE *and* AUDREY

TOUCH.   To-morrow is the joyful day, Audrey; to-morrow will we be
married.

AUD.   I do desire it with all my heart; and I hope it is no dishonest desire to desire to be a woman of the world.[1] Here come two of the
banished Duke's pages.

Enter two Pages

FIRST PAGE.   Well met, honest gentleman.
TOUCH.   By my troth, well met. Come, sit, sit, and a song.
SEC. PAGE.   We are for you: sit i' the middle.
FIRST PAGE.   Shall we clap into 't roundly,[2] without hawking or spit-
ting or saying we are hoarse, which are the only prologues to a bad
voice?
SEC. PAGE.   I' faith, i' faith; and both in a tune, like two gipsies on a
horse.

SONG

It was a lover and his lass,[3]
  With a hey, and a ho, and a hey nonino,
That o'er the green corn-field did pass
  In the spring time, the only pretty ring time,[4]

When birds do sing, hey ding a ding, ding:
Sweet lovers love the spring.

Between the acres of the rye,[5]
  With a hey, and a ho, and a hey nonino,
These pretty country folks would lie,
  In spring time, &c.

[1]*a woman of the world*] a married woman. Cf. *Much Ado*, II, i, 287. In *All's Well*, I, iii,
18, "To go *to the world*" means "to get married."
[2]*clap into 't roundly*] strike up the song straight away. Cf. *Much Ado*, III, iv, 38: "*Clap's
into 'Light o' love.*'"
[3]*seq. It was a lover, etc.*] The music of this song is found with the words in a volume of
MS. music in the Advocates' Library, Edinburgh, which seems to date from the early
part of the seventeenth century.
[4]*ring time*] The Folios read *rang time*, for which the Edinburgh MS. of the song substitutes *ring time, i.e.,* wedding time, which is obviously right.
[5]*Between the acres of the rye*] The reference seems to be to balks or banks of un-
ploughed turf which, in the common-field system of agriculture prevailing in
Elizabethan England, divided the acre strips of land from one another.

This carol they began that hour,
    With a hey, and a ho, and a hey nonino,
How that a life was but a flower
    In spring time, &c.

And therefore take the present time,
    With a hey, and a ho, and a hey nonino;
For love is crowned with the prime
    In spring time, &c.

TOUCH.   Truly, young gentlemen, though there was no great matter in the ditty, yet the note was very untuneable.[6]

FIRST PAGE.   You are deceived, sir: we kept time, we lost not our time.

TOUCH.   By my troth, yes; I count it but time lost to hear such a foolish song. God buy you;[7] and God mend your voices! Come, Audrey.   [*Exeunt.*

SCENE IV. *The Forest.*

Enter DUKE SENIOR, AMIENS, JAQUES, ORLANDO, OLIVER, *and* CELIA

DUKE S.   Dost thou believe, Orlando, that the boy
    Can do all this that he hath promised?

ORL.   I sometimes do believe, and sometimes do not;
    As those that fear they hope, and know they fear.[1]

Enter ROSALIND, SILVIUS, *and* PHEBE

ROS.   Patience once more, whiles our compact is urged:
    You say, if I bring in your Rosalind,
    You will bestow her on Orlando here?

DUKE S.   That would I, had I kingdoms to give with her.

ROS.   And you say, you will have her, when I bring her?

---

[6]*untuneable*] This is the reading of the Folios, for which Theobald substituted *untimeable*. The change seems hardly necessary. "Out of *tune*" and "out of *time*" meant precisely the same thing.

[7]*God buy you*] God be with you. Cf. III, ii, 242.

[1]*fear they hope, and know they fear*] This, the original reading, has been often questioned, but no satisfactory substitute has been suggested. Orlando seeks to express the extremity of his perplexity between hope and fear; he would seem to compare his lot with those who have grave misgivings about what they hope, and their only sure knowledge is that they have misgivings.

ORL. That would I, were I of all kingdoms king.
Ros. You say, you'll marry me, if I be willing?
PHE. That will I, should I die the hour after.
Ros. But if you do refuse to marry me,
 You'll give yourself to this most faithful shepherd?
PHE. So is the bargain.
Ros. You say, that you'll have Phebe, if she will?
SIL. Though to have her and death were both one thing.
Ros. I have promised to make all this matter even.
 Keep you your word, O Duke, to give your daughter;
 You yours, Orlando, to receive his daughter:
 Keep your word, Phebe, that you'll marry me,
 Or else refusing me, to wed this shepherd:
 Keep your word, Silvius, that you'll marry her,
 If she refuse me: and from hence I go,
 To make these doubts all even.
       [*Exeunt* ROSALIND *and* CELIA.
DUKE S. I do remember in this shepherd boy
 Some lively touches of my daughter's favour.
ORL. My lord, the first time that I ever saw him
 Methought he was a brother to your daughter:
 But, my good lord, this boy is forest-born,
 And hath been tutor'd in the rudiments
 Of many desperate studies by his uncle,
 Whom he reports to be a great magician,
 Obscured in the circle of this forest.

Enter TOUCHSTONE *and* AUDREY

JAQ. There is, sure, another flood toward,[2] and these couples are coming to the ark. Here comes a pair of very strange beasts, which in
 all tongues are called fools.
TOUCH. Salutation and greeting to you all!
JAQ. Good my lord, bid him welcome: this is the motley-minded gentleman that I have so often met in the forest: he hath been a
 courtier, he swears.
TOUCH. If any man doubt that, let him put me to my purgation. I
 have trod a measure; I have flattered a lady; I have been politic
 with my friend, smooth with mine enemy; I have undone three
 tailors; I have had four quarrels, and like to have fought one.
JAQ. And how was that ta'en up?

---

[2]*toward*] imminent. Cf. *Hamlet*, V, ii, 356–357: "O proud death, What feast is *toward*
in thine eternal cell."

TOUCH. Faith, we met, and found the quarrel was upon the seventh cause.[3]

JAQ. How seventh cause? Good my lord, like this fellow.

DUKE S. I like him very well.

TOUCH. God 'ild you,[4] sir; I desire you of the like. I press in here, sir, amongst the rest of the country copulatives, to swear and to forswear; according as marriage binds and blood breaks: a poor virgin, sir, an ill-favoured thing, sir, but mine own; a poor humour of mine, sir, to take that that no man else will: rich honesty dwells like a miser, sir, in a poor house; as your pearl in your foul oyster.

DUKE S. By my faith, he is very swift and sententious.

TOUCH. According to the fool's bolt, sir, and such dulcet diseases.[5]

JAQ. But, for the seventh cause; how did you find the quarrel on the seventh cause?

TOUCH. Upon a lie seven times removed:—bear your body more seeming, Audrey:—as thus, sir. I did dislike[6] the cut of a certain courtier's beard: he sent me word, if I said his beard was not cut well, he was in the mind it was: this is called the Retort Courteous. If I sent him word again "it was not well cut," he would send me word, he cut it to please himself: this is called the Quip Modest. If again "it was not well cut," he disabled my judgement: this is called the Reply Churlish. If again "it was not well cut," he would answer, I spake not true: this is called the Reproof Valiant. If again "it was not well cut," he would say, I lie: this is called the Countercheck Quarrelsome: and so to the Lie Circumstantial and the Lie Direct.

JAQ. And how oft did you say his beard was not well cut?

TOUCH. I durst go no further than the Lie Circumstantial, nor he durst not give me the Lie Direct; and so we measured swords and parted.

JAQ. Can you nominate in order now the degrees of the lie?

---

[3]*seventh cause*] This is explained at line 65, *infra*, as "a lie seven times removed." The duel ordinarily was caused by a quarrel in which one man gave the other the lie. Touchstone distinguishes, *infra*, seven modes in which a lie may be given, ranging from the "Retort Courteous" to the "Lie Direct." Shakespeare drew very literally this account of such gradations of the lie from the popular handbook on the subject of fencing and duelling by Vincent Saviolo, an Italian fencing master of London, whose work, called "Vincentio Saviolo his Practise," was published in 1595.

[4]*God 'ild you*] God reward you. See footnote 8 on III, iii, 65, *supra*.

[5]*dulcet diseases*] Probably this is intentional nonsense with some such suggestion as "charming disagreeablenesses." Johnson too seriously proposed to read *discourses* for *diseases*.

[6]*dislike*] The word is often used, as here, not merely for entertaining, but also for expressing, dislike. Cf. *Meas. for Meas.*, I, ii, 17: "I never heard any soldier *dislike* it."

TOUCH.   O sir, we quarrel in print, by the book;[7] as you have books for
   good manners:[8] I will name you the degrees. The first, the Retort
   Courteous; the second, the Quip Modest; the third, the Reply
   Churlish; the fourth, the Reproof Valiant; the fifth, the Countercheck Quarrelsome; the sixth, the Lie with Circumstance; the seventh, the Lie Direct. All these you may avoid but the Lie Direct;
   and you may avoid that too, with an If. I knew when seven justices
   could not take up a quarrel, but when the parties were met themselves, one of them thought but of an If, as, "If you said so, then I
   said so"; and they shook hands and swore brothers. Your If is the
   only peace-maker; much virtue in If.

JAQ.   Is not this a rare fellow, my lord? he's as good at any thing and
   yet a fool.

DUKE S.   He uses his folly like a stalking-horse[9] and under the pre-
   sentation of that he shoots his wit.

Enter HYMEN, ROSALIND, *and* CELIA

Still Music

HYM.   Then is there mirth in heaven,
         When earthly things made even
             Atone together.
         Good Duke, receive thy daughter:
         Hymen from heaven brought her,
             Yea, brought her hither,
         That thou mightst join her hand[10] with his
         Whose heart within his bosom is.

ROS.   To you I give myself, for I am yours.
         To you I give myself, for I am yours.

DUKE S.   If there be truth in sight, you are my daughter.

ORL.   If there be truth in sight, you are my Rosalind.

PHE.   If sight and shape be true,
         Why then, my love adieu!

ROS.   I'll have no father, if you be not he:
         I'll have no husband, if you be not he:
         Nor ne'er wed woman, if you be not she.

[7]*by the book*] An allusion probably to the book by Saviolo mentioned in footnote 3 on
   line 49, *supra.*
[8]*books for good manners*] There were many such. Cf. Hugh Rhodes' *Boke of Nurture,*
   or *Schole of good Manners* (1550?), and Sir Thomas Hoby's *The Courtyer* (1561).
[9]*stalking-horse*] Cf. Drayton's *Polyolbion,* Song 25: "One underneath his horse to get a
   shoot doth *stalk.*"
[10]*her hand*] This is the reading of the Third and Fourth Folios. The First and Second
   Folios read *his hand,* obviously in error.

HYM.   Peace, ho! I bar confusion:
   'T is I must make conclusion
  Of these most strange events:
  Here's eight that must take hands
  To join in Hymen's bands,
   If truth holds true contents.
  You and you no cross shall part:
  You and you are heart in heart:
  You to his love must accord,
  Or have a woman to your lord:
  You and you are sure together,
  As the winter to foul weather.
  Whiles a wedlock-hymn we sing,
  Feed yourselves with questioning;
  That reason wonder may diminish,
  How thus we met, and these things finish.

SONG

  Wedding is great Juno's crown:
   O blessed bond of board and bed!
  'T is Hymen peoples every town;
   High wedlock then be honoured:
  Honour, high honour and renown,
  To Hymen, god of every town!

DUKE S.   O my dear niece, welcome thou art to me!
  Even daughter, welcome, in no less degree.
PHE.   I will not eat my word, now thou art mine;
  Thy faith my fancy to thee doth combine.

Enter JAQUES DE BOYS[11]

JAQ. DE B.   Let me have audience for a word or two:
  I am the second son of old Sir Rowland,
  That bring these tidings to this fair assembly.
  Duke Frederick, hearing how that every day
  Men of great worth resorted to this forest,
  Address'd a mighty power; which were on foot,
  In his own conduct, purposely to take
  His brother here and put him to the sword:
  And to the skirts of this wild wood he came;
  Where meeting with an old religious man,
  After some question with him, was converted
  Both from his enterprise and from the world;

[11]*Jaques de Boys*] See footnote 2 on I, i, 4.

His crown bequeathing to his banish'd brother,
And all their lands restored to them[12] again
That were with him exiled. This to be true,
I do engage my life.

DUKE S.   Welcome, young man;
Thou offer'st fairly to thy brothers' wedding:
To one his lands withheld; and to the other
A land itself at large, a potent dukedom.
First, in this forest let us do those ends
That here were well begun and well begot:
And after, every of this happy number,
That have endured shrewd[13] days and nights with us,
Shall share the good of our returned fortune,
According to the measure of their states.
Meantime, forget this new-fallen dignity,
And fall into our rustic revelry.
Play, music! And you, brides and bridegrooms all,
With measure heap'd in joy, to the measures fall.

JAQ.   Sir, by your patience. If I heard you rightly,
The Duke hath put on a religious life
And thrown into neglect the pompous court?

JAQ. DE B.   He hath.

JAQ.   To him will I: out of these convertites
There is much matter to be heard and learn'd.
[*To Duke S.*] You to your former honour I bequeath;
Your patience and your virtue well deserves it:
[*To Orl.*] You to a love, that your true faith doth merit:
[*To Oli.*] You to your land, and love, and great allies:
[*To Sil.*] You to a long and well-deserved bed:
[*To Touch.*] And you to wrangling; for thy loving voyage
Is but for two months victuall'd. So, to your pleasures:
I am for other than for dancing measures.

DUKE S.   Stay, Jaques, stay.

JAQ.   To see no pastime I: what you would have
I'll stay to know at your abandon'd cave.   [*Exit.*

DUKE S.   Proceed, proceed: we will begin these rites,
As we do trust they'll end, in true delights.   [A *dance.*

---

[12]*them*] This is Rowe's correction of the original reading *him*.
[13]*shrewd*] evil, disastrous. Cf. *Merch. of Ven.*, III, ii, 246: "There are some *shrewd* contents in yon same paper."

EPILOGUE

Ros.   It is not the fashion to see the lady the epilogue; but it is no
more unhandsome than to see the lord the prologue. If it be true
that good wine needs no bush,[1] 't is true that a good play needs no
epilogue: yet to good wine they do use good bushes; and good
plays prove the better by the help of good epilogues. What a case
am I in then, that am neither a good epilogue, nor cannot insinu-
ate with you in the behalf of a good play! I am not furnished like
a beggar, therefore to beg will not become me: my way is to con-
jure you; and I'll begin with the women. I charge you, O women,
for the love you bear to men, to like as much of this play as please
you: and I charge you, O men, for the love you bear to women, —
as I perceive by your simpering, none of you hates them, — that between you and the women the play may please. If I were a woman[2]
I would kiss as many of you as had beards that pleased me, com-
plexions that liked me and breaths that I defied not: and, I am
sure, as many as have good beards or good faces or sweet breaths
will, for my kind offer, when I make curtsy, bid me farewell.

[Exeunt.

---

[1]*bush*] It was customary for tavern-keepers and vintners to hang a *bush* of holly or ivy
outside their houses, usually attached to the signboard.
[2]*If I were a woman*] The part of Rosalind, according to the practice of the Elizabethan
stage, was played by a boy.